Enid put her arms around Elizabeth. "Hey," she said softly, "don't torture yourself. It isn't your fault that your parents are separating. Will you trust me on this one? However terrible the things you may have done seem to you right now, they aren't the cause," Enid insisted.

Elizabeth sighed. Enid just didn't understand. "I guess you're right," she muttered.

"I *know* I'm right," Enid said confidently. "There's no way their separation was your fault. You have to stop thinking like that."

Elizabeth nodded glumly. Of course Enid would say those things—that was what best friends were for. But deep down, Elizabeth knew she was at least partly to blame for her parents' separation, and nothing was going to convince her otherwise.

Bantam Books in the Sweet Valley High Series
Ask your bookseller for the books you have missed

SWEET VALLEY HIGH

WHO'S TO BLAME?

Written by
Kate William

Created by
FRANCINE PASCAL

BANTAM BOOKS
NEW YORK · TORONTO · LONDON · SYDNEY · AUCKLAND

RL 6, IL age 12 and up

WHO'S TO BLAME?
A Bantam Book / July 1990

Sweet Valley High is a registered trademark of Francine Pascal

Conceived by Francine Pascal

Produced by Daniel Weiss Associates, Inc.
33 West 17th Street
New York, NY 10011

Cover art by James Mathewuse

ISBN 0-553-28555-6

Published simultaneously in the United States and Canada

Bantam Books are published by Bantam Books, a division of Bantam Doubleday
Dell Publishing Group, Inc. Its trademark, consisting of the words "Bantam
Books" and the portrayal of a rooster, is Registered in U.S. Patent and Trademark
Office and in other countries. Marca Registrada. Bantam Books, 666 Fifth Avenue,
New York, New York 10103.

PRINTED IN THE UNITED STATES OF AMERICA

OPM   0 9 8 7 6 5 4 3 2 1

To Hilary Bloom

One

"Liz?"

Elizabeth Wakefield heard a voice calling her through the closed bedroom door. She sat up sleepily and rubbed her eyes. But before she could focus on her alarm clock, the door burst open, and her twin sister, Jessica, rushed into the room.

"What are you doing still in bed?" Jessica cried accusingly. "It's almost ten-thirty!"

"You're kidding." Elizabeth groaned. She had set her alarm for nine o'clock, but obviously she had slept through it.

"You'd better hurry up and get dressed," Jessica added. "Daddy finished packing his stuff

1

half an hour ago. We've all eaten breakfast, too."

Elizabeth's heart sank. Now she knew why she had overslept. She had been deep in the middle of a wonderful dream about her family. In the dream, her parents had been holding hands and laughing. They told Elizabeth, Jessica, and their older brother, Steven, that they weren't separating after all.

Elizabeth swung her tanned legs over the side of the bed and reached listlessly for her bathrobe. Too bad it was only a dream! Now that she was awake, she would have to face reality. It was the first day of the month, and her father was moving into an apartment downtown.

"You don't have to act like you're going to a funeral," Jessica said. "It's not the end of the world. Dad's only going to be a few miles away. We can visit him whenever we want to, and he's going to take us out to dinner and do things with us all the time. I think it'll be kind of fun."

Elizabeth stared uncomprehendingly at her sister. Sometimes she couldn't believe she and Jessica were even *related*, let alone identical twins. But the two girls *were* identical. Both had long, blond hair and perfect size-six figures. They both even had identical dimples in their left cheeks that showed whenever they smiled. But Elizabeth's dimple hadn't been showing much

2

lately. Ever since her parents had started to have problems, Elizabeth had been unhappy. Now that they had decided to separate, she was miserable. She loved her family more than anything, and she hated to see it falling apart.

The fact that Jessica looked at the situation differently was hardly surprising—Elizabeth and Jessica were as different on the inside as they were identical on the outside. Elizabeth was sensitive and thoughtful; she was the kind of person other people came to with their problems. Jessica, on the other hand, was about as sensitive as a bass drum. She loved adventure and excitement—and made sure she had plenty of both. Sometimes Jessica thought Elizabeth was a little too predictable, and sometimes Elizabeth thought Jessica was a bit too impulsive.

Elizabeth couldn't remember ever feeling more distant from Jessica than she had since her parents' shocking decision to live apart while they tried to resolve their differences. For Elizabeth, it felt as though someone had dropped a bomb on their house. She had always believed that whatever happened, the Wakefields would weather it together. Over the past month or two, though, Elizabeth had watched her parents drift farther and farther apart.

Jessica had insisted almost from the first fight between their parents that everything was going to be fine. She refused to recognize the seriousness of their problem, and even after her parents had decided to split up, Jessica was acting as if it were no big deal.

Elizabeth sighed and walked over to her chest of drawers. After getting some underwear, she went over to her closet and grabbed chinos and a sweater. In a way, she couldn't really blame Jessica, she thought as she put the clothes on her bed. In a situation like this, who knew how to act or what to feel?

"Where's Mom?" Elizabeth asked Jessica suddenly. It would be hard enough for the twins and Steven to watch their father pack up his things and leave. But for their mother . . .

"She left for the office an hour ago," Jessica said abruptly. "Pretty rude, huh? Especially since Daddy's been on her case about working so many hours for the past month." Jessica frowned. "I think the least she could've done was wait till he left."

Elizabeth shook her head. "She probably wouldn't have been able to take it," she said quietly.

Jessica shrugged. "She should still be here," she insisted. "Anyway, hurry up—we're packing the car!"

Ten minutes later Elizabeth walked into the garage. She was surprised by the big stack of bags and boxes gathered there. Mr. Wakefield had turned his car around so the back was close to the kitchen door, and Steven was helping him load things into the trunk. Though he was a freshman at the nearby state university, Steven had been spending as much time at home lately as possible, especially now that his parents had decided to separate.

A lump formed in Elizabeth's throat as she watched them pack the car. *You'd never guess that Dad is old enough to be Steven's father*, Elizabeth thought. Both had dark hair and eyes, broad shoulders, and nice smiles. Steven looked grown-up for his age, and Ned Wakefield still looked young. *Young and handsome*, Elizabeth thought with a pang. *Think of all the women who are going to want to date him once they know he and Mom have separated!* The thought made her feel miserable.

"Hi, Liz," Mr. Wakefield said, giving her a hug. "Hey," he added softly, rumpling her hair a little, "don't look so sad, sweetie. You know you can't get rid of me this easily, don't you?"

Elizabeth didn't answer. She didn't know that for sure. She didn't know anything anymore!

"Listen, clones, are you going to help load the trunk, or are you just going to stand there and watch us do all the work?" Steven demanded.

Elizabeth smiled, despite herself. Steven had been calling her and Jessica clones for years.

Even at the age of eighteen, he still teased them the way he had when he was eight years old!

But Elizabeth's smile faded as she helped Jessica lift a box into the trunk. In it she spotted a few of her father's legal textbooks that he usually kept in the study. It seemed as though he was taking everything he owned. What was it going to be like without her father in the house? And what if he never came back?

"I know you haven't had breakfast yet, Liz," Mr. Wakefield said, interrupting her thoughts. "Why don't you grab a muffin from the kitchen? I'd like the three of you to follow me downtown in Steve's car. That way you'll see my place, and you'll know where I am." He patted her on the shoulder. "And you won't have any excuses not to come visit right away."

Blinking back tears, Elizabeth nodded. It was really happening. Her father hadn't changed his mind, and it didn't appear that he was going to anytime soon.

Jessica was the only one who was talking during the drive downtown. Steven was concentrating on trailing Mr. Wakefield's car, and Elizabeth sat looking out the window, absorbed in her own sad thoughts.

But Jessica chattered on and on. "Dad's handling all of this so well. Can you believe it, with all the pressure that's on him? I mean, not only did he have to deal with the Santelli trial and everything, but running for mayor . . ."

Elizabeth leaned her head against the window and tried to shut out Jessica's voice. She still couldn't believe her father was serious about running for mayor. For Elizabeth, his decision was so wrapped up in his arguments with Mrs. Wakefield that it was hard to know what to think.

It had all started a month or so ago, when the Wakefields were supporting Peter Santelli for mayor. Mr. Santelli, the father of Maria Santelli, one of the twins' friends at Sweet Valley High, had had a successful career as Sweet Valley's planning commissioner. His race for mayor had been going well until an unidentified source "leaked" an allegation to a local paper that Mr. Santelli had accepted bribes while in office.

All of this had come at a time when Ned Wakefield's interest in his law career was at an all-time low—and Mrs. Wakefield's career as an interior designer was just beginning to soar.

When Mr. Wakefield had decided to defend Peter Santelli in the public trial following the accusations of bribery, the whole family had been behind him. But the judge had dismissed the case due to lack of evidence, and Mr. Wakefield had been devastated. Not long afterward, when some local businessmen asked him to run for mayor in Mr. Santelli's place, Mr. Wakefield hadn't known what to do. He had put off making the decision because he wanted to make sure that his family was behind him.

But after a terrible fight with Mrs. Wakefield, which had been the final straw for both of them, he had decided to go ahead and run for office against her wishes.

"Dad's good at handling pressure," Steven said quietly. "But I wouldn't put too much emphasis on it, Jess. He's trying to put on a good front—for our sake."

Jessica frowned. "You and Liz are both so serious," she muttered. "I don't see why you have to make things even worse than they are. Can't you lighten up a little?"

Steven didn't answer. He was concentrating on fitting his car into the one parking space left at the lot Mr. Wakefield had pulled into.

"Is this it?" Elizabeth asked, craning her neck for a better look at the building. She swallowed hard. It was a plain sandstone structure about six stories tall, without much character. She thought of their pretty split-level house, and her heart ached. *Poor Dad*, she thought. *How can he stand this?*

"Wow," Jessica said, jumping out of the car. "This looks cool."

8

Elizabeth and Steven followed her over to their father's car. "Can we help bring things up?" Steven asked.

Mr. Wakefield squinted up at the apartment building, and for just a moment Elizabeth thought his controlled expression would crumple. But he just smiled and nodded. "That would be great. Thanks."

At least having so many boxes to move upstairs took Elizabeth's mind off what was really happening. But before long, the job was done, and they were all standing uncomfortably inside the one-bedroom apartment.

Jessica flashed the chandelier on and off. "Look—you've got one of these really cool dimmers on your light switch," she said brightly.

Steven coughed. "Dad, do you want to go out for some lunch or something?"

Elizabeth guessed how he was feeling. She couldn't bear the thought of leaving her father there. The apartment was all right, but it was nothing special. It certainly didn't look like a home, not with its blank white walls and beige wall-to-wall carpeting.

"Nah," Mr. Wakefield said with a shrug. "I've got some work to do this afternoon. Henry Patman and his friend James Knapp are coming over to talk about the mayoral race, so I'll be plenty busy." He gave each of them a hug.

"Now promise me you three will take good care of one another—and good care of your mother."

No one said anything. Elizabeth was sure she was going to cry. "Daddy—" she began.

But Jessica cut her off. "We'll be fine, Dad," she assured him. "Hey, can we come over and have dinner here sometime soon? Like maybe next week?"

Mr. Wakefield laughed. "Sure thing. But don't forget, I'm not such a hot cook!" His expression grew serious. "I know how hard this is for you—for all of us. But I want you to remember that this is only temporary. And just remember that your mother and I love you very much."

Elizabeth stared hard at a faint stain in the carpet. She didn't want to look up. She was afraid she would burst into tears if she looked at her father.

"Come on, Liz," Jessica said, tugging her arm.

Elizabeth felt frozen. Finally she let her brother and sister half pull her out the door with them. But she knew that as long as she lived, she would never forget the look on her father's face as he stood in the doorway and waved goodbye.

"Hey," Todd said, tipping up Elizabeth's chin and staring deeply into her eyes. "Are you going to tell me what you're thinking, or do I need ESP?"

Elizabeth's eyes filled with tears for what seemed like the hundredth time that day. It was Saturday night, and she and Todd were sitting on the comfortable sofa in the Wilkinses' living room, watching a video and munching on popcorn—or trying to watch a video, anyway.

Elizabeth couldn't do anything except think about how her parents weren't living together anymore.

Todd had been her boyfriend for a long time. They had been through a lot together, including separation when Todd's father was transferred to Vermont, and an eventual breakup when the distance proved too great for them. But since the Wilkinses had returned to Sweet Valley and Todd and Elizabeth had gotten back together, their relationship had been stronger than ever.

Elizabeth felt she could tell Todd anything, but that night she found it hard to put her feelings into words.

"Listen, you don't want to watch this junk," Todd said, switching off the video with the remote control. "Tell me what you're feeling instead."

Elizabeth kept staring blankly at the TV. "You want to know the truth, Todd? What I really feel—way down deep—is guilty."

"What could you possibly have to feel guilty about?" Todd demanded.

11

Elizabeth shook her head. "A lot of stuff. I can't describe it. Never mind," she added impatiently.

She knew she was pushing Todd away, but she didn't want to tell him the terrible truth: her parents' separation was all her fault.

Two

Sunday brunch, one of Elizabeth's favorite family traditions, was a big flop the next day.

It started off all right. Steven and Jessica were making pancakes, and Elizabeth tried to keep busy reading the Sunday newspaper so she wouldn't notice her father's empty place. Then Alice Wakefield came downstairs, looking more like the twins' older sister than their mother, in a pair of blue jeans and a fleece sweatshirt.

"Mmm, something smells good," she said, giving them all a cautious smile. "How are you all doing? Did everyone sleep well?"

"Not bad," Steven said.

"Fine," Elizabeth said, trying to sound cheerful.

"Listen, I have to run over to the office to

13

check some of the fabrics Sal got from the Design Center yesterday," she went on. Sal was one of the people working with Mrs. Wakefield on designing the interior of the new wing at the Sweet Valley Mall.

"Aren't you even going to eat breakfast, Mom?" Elizabeth asked with concern. It appeared to her that her mother had lost weight. The soft lines on her face were more drawn than usual, and there were faint shadows under her eyes.

"I'll grab a doughnut on the way. Will you three be all right here?"

"We'll be fine, Mom," Jessica said. There was a bit of an edge to her voice, but Mrs. Wakefield didn't seem to notice.

"Good. Let's all have an early supper together tonight, OK?"

Jessica waited until her mother pulled the door closed behind her. "No wonder Dad left," she said bitterly. "Mom's so obsessed with that ridiculous project of hers that she doesn't have time for anything else."

"That isn't fair, Jess," Elizabeth said. "Did it ever occur to you that Mom can't stand being around the house with Dad gone? Maybe she just feels like she has to get out of here for a while."

"She's just being selfish," Jessica objected. "I can't believe her. Here Dad's facing one of the

14

biggest challenges of his life, and how much support does she give him?" She shook her head. "It's horrible. As if running for mayor of Sweet Valley isn't a much bigger deal than picking some fabrics and lighting for the inside of the mall!"

"That's a rotten thing to say, Jess," Steven said. "You know that there's a lot more to interior design than just picking fabrics. And you're not exactly one to put down the mall, either. You spend half your life there!"

"Stop it, you two!" Elizabeth cried.

But Jessica and Steven were just warming up. "You don't know what you're talking about," Jessica snapped at her brother. "How could you understand what's going on between Mom and Dad, anyway? You've been off at college the whole time. You think just because you drop in for a weekend here and there that you're the big expert."

"I happen to have been around enough over the past few months to know that this separation isn't all Mom's fault!" Steven shot back.

Jessica glared at him. "Come to think about it, you *have* been hanging around here an awful lot," she went on. "Don't you have a dorm room anymore? I thought you were supposed to be so big and grown-up now."

"Don't start taking things out on me, Jess," Steven said angrily. "This isn't my fault!"

15

"It isn't Dad's fault, either," Elizabeth commented.

Jessica's eyes sparked with anger. "Whose side are you on, anyway?" she demanded, spinning around to confront her twin. "I thought you were taking Mom's side, not Dad's."

"Who says there are sides in any of this?" Elizabeth cried.

Jessica threw the spatula she was holding into the sink. "I don't want any of these stupid pancakes," she muttered. "Anyway, I don't see why everyone has to make such a big deal out of the whole thing. Lots of people I know have parents who have split up, and they're perfectly fine. Lila's parents are divorced. So are Cara's," she added. Cara Walker was one of her best friends and Steven's girlfriend. She looked defiantly from her brother to her sister. "If you two would stop acting like some big tragedy is going on, maybe everything around here could get back to normal!"

Elizabeth stared at her twin. "You know that isn't true—" she began.

But that was the last thing to say to Jessica just then. "Quit sounding so preachy, Liz! How do you know what I know and what I don't?"

And before anyone could say another word, Jessica ran out of the room and up the stairs to her room.

"Whoops," Elizabeth said uneasily. She glanced

16

at Steven. "She's a little touchy these days, isn't she?"

Steven's face clouded over. "I don't think she is," he retorted. "Give her a break, Liz."

Elizabeth's face fell. "I only meant—"

"I don't want any pancakes anymore, either," Steven snapped. And the next thing Elizabeth knew, Steven had stormed out the back door, muttering something about going to see Cara.

Boy, I really handled that well! she thought. She wasn't sure how she'd done it, but she had managed to get her brother and sister mad at each other—and at her. If this kept up, nobody in the family was going to be on speaking terms by the end of the day!

Elizabeth was out of breath from riding her bicycle. It was a long ride over to her friend Enid's house, but Jessica had taken the Fiat Spider that the twins shared, and Elizabeth wanted to spend some time with her best friend.

She and Enid had been friends for years. Elizabeth had felt even closer to Enid since her parents' decision to separate. She wondered if that was because Enid's parents were divorced. Was that why she sometimes felt uncomfortable at the Wilkinses' house when she saw how happy Todd's parents were together?

Enid was waving from the front door. "Hi.

Come on in. I'm cleaning," she said apologetically, pushing back her curly brown hair. "My mom said I couldn't go anywhere until I straightened up my room. Naturally it's taking me all day."

Elizabeth tried to muster up a smile for her friend. As always, just the sight of Enid's face made her feel better.

"Want some ice cream?" Enid asked. When Elizabeth shook her head, Enid added, "I remember the weekend my dad moved out. I ate a whole gallon of chocolate fudge ripple. I don't know which made me feel worse," she added, shaking her head ruefully, "the ice cream, or the fact that he was gone."

"Yeah, well . . . I haven't felt like eating much lately," Elizabeth admitted.

"Poor thing." Enid gave her a hug. "How are things at home? Is your mom all right?"

Elizabeth shrugged. "She seems to be handling it by disappearing. She's been spending a lot of time at the office this weekend." She followed Enid into her bedroom.

"Let me close the door," Enid said, "and you can tell me everything."

But Elizabeth didn't really feel like going over the details. "Enid, I have to ask you something," she said as soon as the door was closed. "Do you think I . . . I don't know how to put this." Elizabeth paused for a moment, considering. "Do you think I'm the sort of person who causes fights?" she finally asked.

"*What?*" Enid stared at her. "Are you kidding?"

Elizabeth shook her head. "No, I'm serious. This morning I practically started World War Three between Jess and Steve. I think there's something weird I'm doing lately that gets people mad at me and at each other."

"Liz, you're one of the most considerate, loving, easy-to-get-along-with people I've ever met," Enid said earnestly. She put down the shirt she was folding and gave her friend an impulsive hug. "Listen, I know how rough it can be when things aren't going well between your parents. When my father moved out, I couldn't sleep, I couldn't study . . ." She shook her head. "But you can't blame yourself, Liz. You have to remember that it's your parents who are having the problems, not you."

Elizabeth bit her lip. "What if I told you that I'm a big part of the reason they're splitting up in the first place?"

Enid's green eyes widened. "I'm sure you're wrong about that. You're just feeling guilty, Liz."

"Yes, I am—and for good reasons, too. Enid, remember when we went to that terrible legal fraternity party and my father had such a rotten time—and afterward he and my mother got into a big fight? I told you about that, didn't I?"

"Yeah," Enid said slowly. "You did. But what does that have to do with *you*?"

"Well, I should've known how bad my dad was feeling and how much that evening would depress him. But I didn't do a single thing to discourage my mother when she suggested going." Elizabeth stared forlornly at her friend. "And that's not even the worst part. I haven't even told you about what happened at Lake Tahoe."

Enid shook her head. "I don't blame you for feeling this way, Liz, but can't you see how crazy it is? Your parents are the only ones who can make things better or worse for themselves. All you can do is be supportive and wait it out."

"But listen to me, Enid!" Elizabeth cried. "I still haven't told you the worst thing I did."

"OK," Enid said. "Tell me." She sat down on the bed beside Elizabeth.

"I was afraid my mom wasn't going to come to Tahoe with us. She was so busy working on her project, and she started hinting that she might only come for part of the weekend, or not at all." Elizabeth momentarily put her face in her hands, then looked up again. "A few days before we were supposed to leave on the trip, Julia, my mom's assistant, called up with a question for her. I said something to her about Tahoe, about how it would be great for my

20

mom to get away. She said she didn't think the group could do without Mom for a weekend. Enid, you know what a big deal that trip has always been for our family! So I convinced Julia to urge Mom to go. I told her I'd give her the phone number of the inn. She promised only to use it if there was a real emergency."

"Well?" Enid gave her a questioning look. "That still doesn't sound like a big deal to me. You were only trying to keep your parents together by making sure your mother didn't back out of the trip."

"Well, it sure backfired," Elizabeth said. "Because people from the office started calling Mom, and Dad went crazy! Then there *was* some emergency, and she had to leave the mountains anyway, after all my efforts to get her there!" She hung her head. "I should never have given that phone number to Julia. It's the stupidest thing I've ever done."

Enid put her arms around Elizabeth. "Hey," she said softly, "don't torture yourself. It isn't your fault that your parents are separating. Will you trust me on this one? However terrible the things you may have done seem to you right now, they just aren't the cause," Enid insisted.

Elizabeth sighed. Enid just didn't understand. "I guess you're right," she muttered.

"I *know* I'm right," Enid said confidently.

"There's no way their separation was your fault. You have to stop thinking like that."

Elizabeth nodded glumly. Of course Enid would say those things—that was what best friends were for. But deep down, Elizabeth knew she was at least partly to blame for her parents' separation, and nothing was going to convince her otherwise.

"Hi, Liz!" Mrs. Wakefield exclaimed, stepping through the back door into the kitchen. She held a bag of groceries in her arms. "Sorry I'm so late. I stopped off at the market."

"That's OK, Mom. I just got home from Enid's," Elizabeth said.

"Where are Jessica and Steve? I got the ingredients to make tacos," Mrs. Wakefield said. It was obvious that she was trying to be cheerful. It was just as obvious that her act wasn't working.

"Jess left a note saying she's going to Lila's house for dinner. And I don't know where Steve is," Elizabeth explained.

"Oh." Mrs. Wakefield's face fell.

"We can eat dinner together, Mom—just you and me," Elizabeth said quickly.

"Sure," her mother said. But she didn't look very happy, and making tacos for two didn't seem like a lot of fun to Elizabeth, either.

"The house feels so quiet," Mrs. Wakefield said when they sat down to eat together at the table. "I wonder"—she drew a shaky breath—"how your father's doing. Do you think he's eating all by himself somewhere?"

Elizabeth felt a lump form in her throat. Was this ever going to get any easier? "I don't know, Mom."

Alice Wakefield's expression was very sad. She toyed with the food on her plate. "I feel like I've made so many mistakes in the past few weeks. Liz, the more I look back on what's happened between your father and me, the more I feel that a lot of it was my fault. If I hadn't overreacted so often, if I hadn't allowed my work to intrude . . ." She shook her head. "Every time I think about that weekend at Tahoe I want to kick myself."

Elizabeth's mouth was dry. "Why?" she asked, dreading the answer.

"I should never have left," her mother said firmly. "That weekend meant a great deal to the whole family, and I don't know what I thought I was doing, letting work get in the way. And I shouldn't have taken any of those phone calls, either. I guess I've learned my lesson the hard way, Liz. My career matters to me, but not enough to let it drive away my husband."

Elizabeth stared at her mother. So she had

been right. If she hadn't given Julia their phone number, those phone calls never could have intruded the way they had. And her mother wouldn't have left the resort.

Elizabeth didn't need to hear another word. Her mother had all but said it: Those phone calls and that ruined weekend had caused her parents' separation.

And whose fault were they in the first place but Elizabeth's?

Three

Jessica made her way through the crowded cafeteria, trying to find Amy Sutton and Lila Fowler. Usually Jessica hated Mondays. Being back at school after the weekend was always a letdown. But since things had been so rough at home, it was a relief to be with her friends instead of her family.

"Hey, Jess!" Amy waved at her, her blond hair swaying.

Jessica slid her tray onto the table, next to her friend's. "Hi, Ame. Hi, Lila." She glanced quickly from one to the other, wondering if they would treat her any differently now that her father had moved out. She hoped not. The last thing Jessica wanted was anyone's pity.

Luckily Lila and Amy were in the middle of an argument about Pi Beta Alpha, the sorority all three girls belonged to. "Jess, tell us what you think. We've got to figure out some kind of party to throw at the end of the month. We haven't had a sorority party in ages. Don't you think we should have a formal dance?" Lila asked.

Amy wrinkled her nose. "No way. We want something fun and casual."

Jessica's eyes brightened. "A Pi Beta Alpha party would be the perfect place for me to invite Charlie."

Lila and Amy looked at each other and groaned in unison. "Not again," Lila said.

Jessica raised her eyebrows. "You two are so immature," she said loftily. "If you're going to start bugging me again just because neither of you has met this guy—"

"More to the point, *you* haven't met him, Jessica," Amy interrupted with a giggle.

Jessica shrugged. "I know you're jealous. You probably wish *you* had a wonderful guy calling you up all the time, telling you how great you are."

"Actually, I prefer to see my dates in person," Lila said, snickering. "That way I know they *exist*."

Jessica refused to let them get to her. She thought the way she had met Charlie was incredibly romantic. Just because Amy and Lila hadn't been resourceful enough to think about using a teen phone line to meet someone new didn't mean she had to listen to their catty remarks!

Jessica had seen the party line advertised on TV. All you had to do was dial the 900 number, and you got connected to a great group of people. She had called and had talked to Charlie, as well as some other people. But before long, she and Charlie were talking all the time—at first on the party line, and then they had finally exchanged home numbers. They'd gotten pretty close, and Jessica really liked Charlie. The only problem was, she hadn't met him yet—not in person, anyway.

Not that Charlie didn't want to meet. He always sounded just as eager as Jessica did when they talked about getting together. And he didn't live that far away, either. He lived in a nearby town. But Charlie hadn't been able to go out any of the times Jessica had suggested.

"You'll see," Jessica said stubbornly to Lila. "Charlie will come through. And even if it's taking us a while to get together, it'll be worth waiting for!"

"Good," Lila said, unwrapping her ice cream bar and taking a bite. "Just make sure he has a couple of cute friends for Amy and me." She shook her head. "I can't believe I'm saying this, but the way things have been going around here lately, I think both of us could stand being fixed up!"

Jessica got home later than she had planned Monday afternoon. As co-captain of the cheerleading squad, she had to stay at practice until the end, and she had had to arrange a scheduling meeting with the cheerleaders after practice. She had planned on asking one of her friends for a ride home, since Elizabeth had the Fiat. But she had had to go back into the school to pick up a book, and when she came outside, all the cheerleaders had left. The bus seemed to take forever, and it was almost six o'clock when she opened the front door of the Wakefield house.

"Hi, everyone! I'm home!" she called.

"It's only me, Jessica!" Alice Wakefield called back from the kitchen. "Your brother went back to school this morning, and Liz is upstairs."

Jessica wandered into the kitchen. "Oh." She sniffed the air. "Smells good, Mom. What are you making?"

"Just some soup," Mrs. Wakefield said. Her eyes were puffy, and Jessica wondered if she had been crying.

"Mom, are you all right?"

"I'm just tired. We had a long day of meetings, and I'm feeling a little under the weather."

Jessica nodded. "I thought so. You didn't even bring the mail inside," she said accusingly, dumping a pile of letters on the counter.

Mrs. Wakefield flipped through them. "Yuck," she said. "Nothing but bills. Oh, good," she added absently. "I've been waiting for this." She tore open a yellow envelope that Jessica recognized as the phone bill. Her stomach sank. "Your father and I were trying to estimate monthly expenses, and—" Mrs. Wakefield's eyes widened in astonishment. "What?" she cried, staring at the bill. "This is crazy. There must be some kind of mistake. We've never had a bill this big before!"

"Uh, is it really big?" Jessica asked nervously. "Maybe they got us mixed up with somebody else. That happened to Lila once," she added quickly. "Some weirdo was calling Japan and giving the Fowlers' phone card number, and they got a bill for six hundred dollars."

"Well, ours isn't far behind," Mrs. Wakefield said grimly. "Three hundred and seventy-five dollars!"

Jessica winced. That was a lot worse than she had been expecting. "Wow," she said, trying to sound innocent. "I wonder why it's so big?"

Jessica had been dreading this moment for weeks, ever since she found out how much the

29

party line cost. But she didn't see any reason to let her mother know the huge phone bill was her fault. At least not before she had to.

"I don't understand this. What are all these nine hundred numbers? Isn't a nine hundred number a party line of some sort?" Mrs. Wakefield continued.

To Jessica's dismay Elizabeth chose just that moment to walk into the kitchen. There was no way Jessica was going to be able to lie to her mother in front of her sister, especially since Elizabeth knew exactly what she'd been up to and why the phone bill was so enormous!

"Uh, party line?" Jessica echoed, trying not to look guilty. "What do you mean?"

"Liz, do you know anything about this? You haven't been using a nine hundred number, have you?" Mrs. Wakefield asked.

Elizabeth shook her head and looked straight at Jessica.

"Uh, Mom," Jessica began uncomfortably. "See, there was this teen line that I kind of started to use a little bit, and—"

"Teen line? Jessica, what's going on here?" Mrs. Wakefield demanded.

Jessica nervously chewed on a fingernail. "OK, I admit it. I've been calling up one of the nine hundred numbers—or at least I was for a few weeks last month. But that was before I knew how much money it cost. I swear, Mom, I'd never have done it if I'd known it would cost so much!"

Alice Wakefield was furious. "How could you possibly do something so irresponsible, Jessica? Honestly, I don't know what you could have been thinking of. These calls cost a fortune!" She scanned the bill. "Eleven dollars on the eighth . . . fourteen dollars on the ninth . . . Jessica, this is ridiculous!"

Jessica shifted uncomfortably. "I told you, Mom, I didn't know how expensive it was at first. The minute I found out, I stopped calling." She stared defensively at her mother, unwilling to let herself be put in a bad light. Then suddenly she had a brainstorm. *Maybe there's a way to get out of this!*

"Besides, I only started calling the party line in the first place because I was lonely," Jessica protested, crossing her arms. "I didn't have anyone to talk to—and you and Daddy were so busy fighting with each other that I couldn't even turn to you guys." *There*, Jessica thought defiantly.

But her mother didn't look very impressed. "Jessica, blaming something like this on your father and me isn't fair, and you know it. The fact is, I don't like your attitude at all. It's bad enough being irresponsible and running up a huge bill, but trying to hide it and blame it on others is even worse." She frowned as she studied the bill. "It looks to me like you've run up almost three hundred dollars of phone calls here. I'll use my calculator to figure it out to the penny. And until you've paid me back, I'm suspending your allowance. I'll use that money for the bill."

Jessica felt her heart sink. No allowance? How was she supposed to survive?

Her mother seemed to be reading her mind. "You may just have to get a part-time job until this debt is repaid," she said calmly.

Jessica didn't answer. She could never remember feeling so betrayed. How could her mother possibly treat her so unfairly?

Daddy would never do this to me, Jessica thought. *Daddy would understand.*

Her mood lifted a little as she watched her mother begin to set the table. Maybe it wouldn't be such a bad idea to let her father know how unfairly she was being punished. If anyone could intervene on her behalf, it was her father!

"This is a pleasant surprise!" Ned Wakefield exclaimed, getting up from the chair behind his desk in his office downtown.

It was Tuesday afternoon, and Jessica had dropped by her father's law office unannounced.

"Hi, Dad," Jessica said, leaning over his desk to give him a kiss. "I just thought I'd come in and see how you're doing." She glanced at the stack of papers on his desk. "How's the race for mayor? Are you winning?"

Mr. Wakefield laughed. "I'd say that's a little premature, Jess. But it's been fairly time consuming." He sighed. "Which, under the circumstances, is a good thing. I miss you guys a lot." He looked straight at her. "How are things going at home? Is everything OK?"

Jessica twisted a lock of hair. "Well, actually, Mom's mad at me. I'm being punished," she said dramatically.

"Really? Why?"

Jessica cleared her throat. She was prepared. She had rehearsed the story a few times. "I guess I was pretty irresponsible about the phone last month. I found this great teen phone line— you know, one of those nine hundred numbers— and started using it before I knew how expensive it was. And you know, with everything going on between you and Mom . . . well, I didn't realize how lonely I was and how much I needed to turn to the new friends I made through the party line," she said. Just talking this way made Jessica feel so sorry for herself, she could have cried. "Mom's furious, though. She wants me to pay back every penny, and she says I won't get any allowance until I do."

"That sounds a little harsh," Mr. Wakefield

said. "Maybe I should give your mother a call and talk it over with her."

Jessica smiled. "Daddy, would you do that for me? That would be great."

"I think parents can be a little too strict sometimes—especially when there's only one of them around and they can't bounce ideas off each other. Don't worry," her father added. "I'll straighten it out."

Jessica gave him a hug. "You're the best father in the whole world," she said in a muffled voice.

She meant it, too. Until Jessica dropped by his office that afternoon, she hadn't realized how much she missed him. "It's rotten at home without you," she said suddenly.

Mr. Wakefield tightened his arms around her. "I love you, Jess. Take care of yourself, and don't let things at home upset you. It'll be all right."

Jessica felt a sudden pang. What if her parents got divorced and her father moved far away? She couldn't bear it. She would go wherever he went, she decided. She could be like Lila, who lived alone with her father and got everything she wanted. And if Mr. Wakefield was elected mayor of Sweet Valley, the whole town would be hers!

"Daddy, if you and Mom don't get back together, can I come live with you?" Jessica asked impulsively.

Her father stared sadly at her. "Oh, Jess," he said. "Don't start thinking like that."

It occurred to Jessica that what she had said wasn't very tactful. But she didn't care. It was what she was feeling—and she had to look out for herself, didn't she?

Jessica dialed Charlie's number as soon as she got home later that afternoon. She was up in her bedroom with the door closed and the radio on, so nobody could hear her.

"Hi, princess," he said the minute he heard her voice. "Do you have any idea how much I've missed you?"

Jessica felt her heartbeat quicken. She absolutely adored these phone calls with Charlie. He had such a deep, sexy voice. And he always sounded happy to hear from her.

"How come you didn't call me last night? Don't you know how it injures me when I don't hear from you?" he demanded. "I'm glad you called before I expired."

Jessica giggled. Charlie had a great sense of humor. He always made her laugh. "I've missed you, too," she said softly.

She just couldn't understand it. The relationship with Charlie felt so special when they were talking on the phone. She knew how much he liked her, and she knew it was genuine, too.

And she had also taken some risks—and gotten in a lot of trouble—for Charlie's sake. Her mother was furious with her, and she'd lost her allowance, too.

The very least he could do was to ask to meet her—and soon. Jessica was getting tired of conducting a long-distance romance with a boy who lived practically next door!

Four

Wednesday at school Pi Beta Alpha announced the party they had scheduled for two weeks from Friday. It was going to be a costume party, complete with dancing, refreshments, and a prize for the best costumes.

Everyone was talking about the party. It seemed like a long time since there had been a big party or dance at school, and with colorful posters up all over advertising this one, enthusiasm was running high.

"I wonder what I should wear," Jessica said at lunchtime, twirling a lock of her hair.

"Come with Charlie," Amy said and giggled. "You two can dress as phantoms. Or he can come as the Invisible Man!"

Jessica gave her a furious look. "For your information," she said coldly, "Charlie and I have a date this weekend. So quit calling him invisible."

Amy looked impressed. "Really? Where are you going?"

Jessica thought fast. "Roller-skating," she lied.

Amy's eyebrows shot up. "I don't believe it."

"Well, you'd better, because it's true," Jessica shot back.

"Which roller rink are you going to? The one downtown?" Amy demanded.

Jessica took a bite of her salad and stalled for time. "I think so, but we haven't decided when yet," she told Amy.

"Well, as soon as you've decided, tell me. I want to come and check this guy out for myself." Amy gave Jessica a challenging look. "If he's not there, I'm telling everyone in the whole sorority that you just made Charlie up—that he's a phony boyfriend."

Jessica pushed a piece of lettuce around on her plate. Now she would have to make sure Charlie met her on Saturday at the roller rink. If he came up with another one of his excuses, she was ready to tell him it was all over. It was one thing getting her mother mad at her, and she could even stand losing her allowance. But being humiliated by her friends—that was taking things too far!

*   *   *

Elizabeth and Todd had a date planned for that afternoon after school. Todd came by *The Oracle* office, where Elizabeth was hard at work on an article for the school paper.

"Todd Wilkins, Rescue Squad," he said solemnly, flipping open his wallet at her like an FBI agent. "I'm here to whisk you away to a beautiful beach!" He leaned over to kiss her on the tip of her nose, and Elizabeth forced herself to smile.

"Let me just finish up here," she mumbled.

Todd looked over her shoulder at a Pi Beta Alpha poster advertising the costume party. "Hey, have you given any thought to who we should dress up as for the party?" he asked Elizabeth. "How about Bonnie and Clyde? I could wear a fedora and try to look dangerous."

Elizabeth finished the sentence she was revising and closed her notebook. "I hadn't really thought about it yet," she said.

To tell you the truth, a little voice inside her said, *I'm not so sure I want to go at all.*

The whole way to the beach Todd talked about the dance. He had several different ideas for costumes. "We could go as Batman and Cat Woman," he suggested. "Or as the King and Queen of Hearts."

Elizabeth stared out the window. "We'll figure something out," she said absently.

"Or what about going as bookends? We could make a bunch of books out of cardboard and put them in between us, and—"

Elizabeth couldn't stand it anymore. "Todd," she cut him off, "this isn't a costume party for couples only, you know. We don't have to be two of a kind. You can dress up as something, and I could dress as something else. We don't have to *match*."

She hadn't intended to blurt her opinion out so strongly, and from the hurt expression on Todd's face she could tell she had made a real blunder.

"Forget it," Elizabeth said quickly. "I'm just in a bad mood. I don't know why."

Todd gave her a quick glance. "We don't have to go dressed as a couple, Liz. Anyway, we can talk about it some other time. Let's enjoy the afternoon."

But that was easier said than done. They had barely spread out their beach towels when Elizabeth began feeling uneasy again. She just couldn't seem to relax. When Todd put his arm around her, she stiffened.

"You know, I think I've got a headache—that's what my problem is," she said at last, squinting into the sun.

"Then let's get you a cold drink and just head home," Todd said.

Elizabeth felt a wave of relief wash over her.

She wanted nothing more than to go home and see how her mother was doing. She knew she had disappointed Todd, but she couldn't help it. Elizabeth just didn't feel like being with him. She wanted to be at home, in case her mother felt lonely or needed her. Besides, she had a lot more serious things to think about than a silly sorority party!

"Hey, this is a surprise!" Elizabeth exclaimed when her brother walked through the back door at six-thirty on Wednesday evening.

"My last class of the day got canceled, and I decided to come home and see how Mom's doing," Steven said.

Jessica walked into the kitchen. "Oh," she said, seeing Steven. "It's only you. I thought Mom was home." She frowned at him. "Aren't you getting kind of worried that they might kick you out of school if you don't spend more time there?"

Steven made a face at Jessica. "It's nice to see you too, Jess."

Jessica shrugged. "Listen, since you're home, maybe you should think about giving Dad a call. He told me yesterday he hasn't heard from you since he moved out." She seemed to be deliberately baiting Steven, and it was clear she was still angry at him.

Steven looked at her in stony silence.

"Jess, it isn't up to you to tell Steve what to do," Elizabeth put in.

"Yeah, and maybe you ought to think about being a little nicer to Mom," Steven snapped at Jessica. "Do you think running up a huge phone bill is a very good way to help her out right now?"

"Who told you about that?" Jessica cried. "That happens to be between her and me."

Elizabeth put her fingers in her ears. "Cut it out, you two. Mom's going to be home any minute. She doesn't need to hear you guys screaming at each other on top of everything else."

"Oh, quit being such a goody-two-shoes," Jessica retorted. "You always have to get in the middle of every fight, don't you?"

"Don't yell at Liz!" Steven said, furious all over again.

Elizabeth sighed forlornly and leaned back against the kitchen counter. It was hard to believe that they had *ever* gotten along together—or that they ever would again!

To add to the general confusion, the door opened, and Mrs. Wakefield came in, just as the telephone rang. Jessica lunged for it, practically poking out Elizabeth's eye.

"Oh, hi, Daddy," she said breathlessly, shooting an injured look in her brother's direction.

"Steve! What are you doing at home?" Mrs. Wakefield exclaimed. "What a surprise!"

Jessica covered the telephone with her hand. "Dad wants to talk to you, Mom." Under her breath she added to her brother, "See? Even Mom thinks you're hanging around here too much."

Steven sneered at her, but Elizabeth was concentrating on her mother's reaction.

Mrs. Wakefield's eyes lit up. She took the receiver from Jessica, a smile on her face. "Ned? Hi!"

Elizabeth watched her mother expectantly. Maybe this was it. Maybe her father was going to say that the whole separation was a big mistake, that he was coming home.

To her dismay her mother's expression darkened, and she glanced angrily at Jessica. "No, Ned, that is *not* what happened. And I don't think it's appropriate for you to undermine my judgment in this, either. You and I should talk about this later."

Oh, no, Elizabeth thought. *Another argument.*

"Not now, Ned. I just walked through the door. I haven't even had time to take off my coat. And Steve's here, so I'd like to say hello to him. I'll talk to you later about this. *And* to Jessica."

And without another word she hung up the phone.

43

Jessica cleared her throat. "So what's for dinner?"

Mrs. Wakefield glared at her. "Jessica, the next time you go behind my back and tell your father that you've been mistreated around here, I'm warning you . . ."

"But, Mom—" Jessica began.

"We'll talk about it after dinner," Mrs. Wakefield interrupted her.

Steven came over to give his mother a hug. "Hang in there, Mom," he said. He gave Jessica a stern look. "We all have to stick together. The last thing we need now is to start picking fights with each other!"

Jessica's eyes flashed with anger. "Great, so sticking together means that I get my allowance taken away from me and that you can take Mom's side and forget that you even have a father!"

"Jessica, stop it right now," Mrs. Wakefield said wearily.

Elizabeth felt her eyes fill with tears. She didn't know how much longer she was going to be able to take this.

Enid had assured her that things would settle down after Mr. Wakefield moved out. How long was it going to take before the house stopped feeling like a battlefield?

* * *

Jessica slammed her door. It sounded so good, she opened the door and slammed it again. "Take that!" she said, scowling.

As far as she was concerned, her mother and Steven deserved each other. Elizabeth was wimping out, refusing to take sides. Well, Jessica knew where her loyalty lay! If things got any worse, she was going to ask her father if she could move in with him.

She wandered over to her dresser and inspected herself in the mirror. "This much stress isn't good for me," she muttered, checking carefully to make sure she wasn't getting bags under her eyes. She took a deep breath, trying to calm herself before she dialed Charlie's number. This was an important phone call. She didn't want anything to go wrong.

"OK, Charlie Ryan," she whispered to herself, crossing her fingers. "Either you go roller-skating with me on Saturday afternoon, or you're going to lose your telephone girlfriend!"

She dialed his number. Charlie answered on the third ring.

"Hey, Jessica! I was just about to call *you*," he said, sounding so genuinely glad to hear from her that Jessica's confidence went up a dozen notches.

"I must have ESP," Jessica said, giggling. The minute she heard Charlie's voice she felt like her old self again. It was as if all her worries about her parents vanished and everything was going to be all right.

"What are you up to?" Charlie asked.

"Oh, just hanging out. Thinking about you," Jessica added, impressed with her own daring.

"Charlie, listen. I have something to say," she blurted suddenly. "I know you've been busy and I've been busy and we haven't been able to find time to get together yet. But I can't stand not being able to meet you in person. Can we make a date—for sure?"

Charlie coughed. "Sure, Jessica. Whenever you want," he said.

"Saturday," Jessica said promptly. "Saturday afternoon. Let's go roller-skating. We can go out for something to eat afterward," she added, suddenly afraid he wouldn't think it was so-phisticated enough.

After all, Charlie was a pretty cool guy. She could tell just from the way he joked around with her. He was so witty, and he always had a clever comeback.

But if Charlie thought roller-skating was juvenile, he didn't show it. "I'm glad you asked me, Jessica. I've been wanting to meet you for so long. And I can't wait to see you . . . to find out if you look as beautiful as you sound," Charlie said in a husky voice.

Chills ran up and down Jessica's spine. "So

we can meet at the roller rink downtown in Sweet Valley at three o'clock?"

"Sure!" He was quiet for a minute. "Wow, can you believe we're finally going to meet, after all this time?"

"I can't, to tell you the truth." Jessica cleared her throat. She was excited, and a little bit nervous. "How will I know you?" She giggled. "Will you be carrying a red rose?"

Charlie laughed. "Not a bad idea. That's what they always do in old movies, right? Well, three o'clock at the roller rink, look for a handsome young man carrying a red rose, and that'll be me."

This was too good to be true, Jessica thought. She was finally going to meet the man of her dreams—and she would be able to tell Amy Sutton she could come and spy on them all she wanted!

Five

All during English class, Elizabeth was deep in thought. In fact, she felt as if she were a million miles away. Usually English was one of her favorite classes. She loved her teacher, Roger Collins, who was also the faculty adviser for *The Oracle*. He was demanding but fair, and one of the best-liked teachers in the school. Elizabeth had gotten to know him fairly well by working on the newspaper, and she really valued his opinion.

That day Mr. Collins was discussing Shakespeare's tragedy *Othello*. "Can anyone tell me why the love between Othello and Desdemona breaks down in this play?" he asked the class.

Elizabeth propped her chin up on one hand

and stared out the window. A few wispy clouds dotted the bright blue sky. *Why does love ever break down?* she thought sadly. She felt her eyes filling with tears. Suddenly she heard someone say her name.

"Liz?" Mr. Collins was asking, looking right at her.

Elizabeth turned and stared at him. "I'm sorry—I didn't hear the question," she said in a voice not much above a whisper.

A few people snickered. "Never mind," Mr. Collins said. "Someone else, please—anyone. What is the nature of Othello's jealousy?" He gave Elizabeth a look as if to say that even though he had let her off the hook this time, he was well aware that she hadn't been paying attention.

Ten minutes before the bell rang, Mr. Collins stopped the discussion. "I have your essays from last week. With a few exceptions, these reflect some of the best work I've seen from you all year." He grinned. "In short, I'm impressed. So keep it up." He passed the papers back one by one. Elizabeth's was at the bottom of the pile.

"Liz, please see me about this," Mr. Collins had scrawled across the bottom of the essay, where he usually wrote "*A—nice job.*" There was no grade on the paper.

Elizabeth was stunned. She looked anxiously

at the paper. She had been a little preoccupied when she wrote it, but she didn't think it was *that* bad.

She didn't have to wait long for her teacher's reaction. When the bell rang, Mr. Collins motioned for her to stay behind.

"Liz, I'm going to be blunt," he said, sitting down on the edge of his desk and looking straight at her. "I'm very worried about you. You've seemed really far away in class the past few weeks. You weren't even listening to—much less participating in—our discussion today. And, to tell you the truth, this paper seems like a real rush job. It's far below what you're capable of. What's going on?"

Elizabeth shifted in her seat. "I guess I'm . . ." she began, then stopped. She knew this was the perfect moment to tell Mr. Collins that her parents had separated, that there had been a lot of tension at home lately. She knew he would understand and that he might even be able to help her. After all, he was raising a young son alone. But somehow she couldn't bring herself to tell Mr. Collins the truth. Talking about it was still too painful. And it was as if telling him would make the separation more real—and permanent. "I don't know what's wrong with me. I'll try harder next time," she said, hanging her head.

Mr. Collins looked so disappointed in her! It was heartbreaking.

"All right," he said. "Take care of yourself, Liz—you look tired. Why don't you rewrite the paper for next week?"

"OK," Elizabeth agreed.

I can't do anything right, she thought, turning to leave the room. *I messed up everything at home, and now I'm bombing at school, too. Everything I do lately seems to be a disaster.*

She had promised Mr. Collins that she would try harder. But what if she couldn't? What if she couldn't do better no matter *how* hard she tried?

Elizabeth was glad she had ridden her bicycle to school that day. It felt good to get some fresh air after a rough day at school, and she was enjoying just riding around. She felt carefree for the first time in a long while.

She hadn't really planned her route. She ended up cycling through town instead of going directly home. Down one street, up another—until all of a sudden she found herself in front of her father's apartment building.

Elizabeth leaned her bicycle against a tree and shaded her eyes with her hand, squinting up at the building. She had forgotten which window was his. Was it the fourth or fifth from the end?

A tear ran down her cheek. Was her father really going to stay in that little apartment? Didn't he miss them?

She stayed outside the building for a long time—ten minutes, maybe even twenty. She didn't want to be there, but she didn't feel like leaving, either.

By the time Elizabeth got home later that afternoon she was exhausted. In fact, she couldn't ever remember being so tired. Her head was pounding, and she ached all over, as if she were coming down with the flu.

The red light on the answering machine was blinking rapidly, and Prince Albert, the Wakefields' golden retriever, barked his greetings to Elizabeth. Otherwise, the house was perfectly still.

Elizabeth got some fresh water for Prince while she played back the phone messages.

"Liz, it's Todd. I thought we had a date to go shopping. I waited for you by the gym door for twenty minutes, and then I thought I'd call to see if you'd gone home early. Call me as soon as you get in."

Then there was a beep, followed by the next message. "It's me, Todd. Call me."

The next two messages were just little clicks,

indicating that whoever had called had hung up the phone.

"Darn," Elizabeth said to Prince Albert, scratching him behind his ears the way he loved. "I forgot all about meeting Todd. He's going to kill me."

She knew she should jump up right then and call him to apologize and explain, but Elizabeth felt too tired to talk to anybody. She couldn't bring herself to pick up the phone and dial Todd's number.

Just then, the door flew open, and Jessica came bounding in. "Look what I got in the mail!" she cried, waving a big brown envelope from a sweepstakes company. "I'm a lucky prizewinner. I've won a million dollars!"

Elizabeth groaned. "Jessica, they send those things to everybody. You probably haven't won anything."

Jessica's eyes narrowed. "Boy, you're a barrel of laughs lately," she said, yanking open the refrigerator. "There's nothing in here," she complained. "Mom hasn't been shopping in weeks!"

Elizabeth sighed. She was just about to tell Jessica to give their mother a break when the phone rang. She was glad; she didn't want to get into another argument. "Hello?" she said.

"Liz! I'm so glad you're there. I was beginning to worry about you," Todd said, his voice filled with concern.

"Sorry!" Elizabeth said. That came out a little more offhand than she had intended, so she tried again. "I'm sorry, Todd. I forgot we were going shopping. I just totally spaced out."

As soon as Jessica learned the call wasn't for her, she wandered into the living room and turned on the TV.

"I waited for about half an hour," Todd said, "and then I figured something must have come up." Elizabeth could hear the hurt in his voice. "I miss you," he added.

Elizabeth twisted the phone cord around her finger. "I know, Todd," she said.

Todd waited a second. "Where were you?" he asked slowly. "I tried *The Oracle* office and the gym."

"I just went for a bike ride. It was so nice out, I guess I forgot about everything else." She couldn't seem to make herself tell Todd the truth—that she'd been so upset about her parents she didn't feel like being with anyone—not even him.

"Look, Liz, are you mad at me for some reason?" Todd asked suddenly.

"Of course not!" Elizabeth answered. But she could hear the irritation creeping into her voice. She felt that he was pushing her. "Todd, don't take it personally. I just forgot."

He was quiet for a minute. "OK," he finally said. "But I needed your help choosing a birthday present for my mom, remember? What am I going to do now? Her birthday's tomorrow!"

Elizabeth concentrated on the pattern the late-afternoon sun was making on the kitchen floor. "I don't know, Todd. I'm sorry, but I need to stick around here tonight. Mom's going to need help with dinner."

"Sure," Todd said, sounding disappointed again. "I understand. But don't forget your boy-friend needs a little attention once in awhile, too." He made the last comment as if it were a joke, but Elizabeth could tell he meant it. She hadn't been paying any attention to Todd lately.

Elizabeth took a deep breath. "I won't," she said. She was amazed that she actually felt relieved when she hung up the phone. Since when had it been hard to talk to Todd?

What is wrong with me? she thought with agony. Todd was hurt, and it was all her fault. The way things were going, she would probably end up ruining their relationship, too.

Well, better now than later, she said to herself. *No point waiting till we're married—like Mom and Dad. We might as well get it over with now before it gets too painful.*

"You seem a little quiet, Liz. Are you all right?" Mrs. Wakefield asked after dinner that night.

"I'm fine, Mom. I think maybe I'm just coming down with a cold or something," Elizabeth said. Every muscle in her body seemed to ache.

"I guess that means I have to do the dishes again," Jessica said, looking pained.

Elizabeth gave her a dirty look. The number of times Jessica had helped do the dishes in the past month could be counted on the fingers of one hand. She never did her share of work around the house.

Elizabeth was about to tell her twin off when the doorbell rang.

"Why don't you get that, Liz? I'll help Jessica," Mrs. Wakefield said.

Elizabeth walked slowly to the front door. To her surprise, Penny Ayala was standing on the porch, an emerald-green file folder in her hand.

"Hi, Liz. I was just driving home from a music lesson and saw the lights on and wondered if I could talk to you for a couple of minutes."

"Sure. Come on in," Elizabeth said, ushering her into the living room. Penny, a pert, pretty senior, was editor-in-chief of the school newspaper. Elizabeth loved working for her, especially since Penny had let her work on a number of feature articles as well as writing the "Eyes and Ears" gossip column.

"What's up, Penny?" Elizabeth asked as the girls sat down on the couch.

Penny leaned forward, a frown on her pretty

face. "Liz, this is a hard thing for me to say to you. You've always been one of the best staff members—and one of our best writers, too. But— well, lately it seems like you're not all there. I mean, you missed two *Oracle* meetings this month, which isn't like you. And you never showed up for an interview you'd scheduled with Jason Fisherman, the leader of the local chapter of the California Civic Rights group." She shook her head. "Mr. Fisherman called me this afternoon and asked what happened. I felt really bad about it, Liz. Can you tell me why you didn't go?"

This was too much, Elizabeth thought. She had completely forgotten her interview with Mr. Fisherman!

"Oh, Penny, I'm so sorry," she said. She could feel her lips trembling as she fought back tears. "Look . . . I promise it won't happen again. I've just been really preoccupied. . . . There's been a lot of stuff going on at home. I can't talk about it, but you can trust me—I'll be more responsible from now on."

Penny patted her on the arm. "It's not the end of the world, Liz. To tell you the truth, I was just afraid you were getting sick of writing for *The Oracle* and didn't want to do it any-more." She smiled. "I'm glad that's not the case. Listen, don't worry about it. You can reschedule with Mr. Fisherman. I'm sure he'll understand."

Elizabeth took a deep breath. Now she'd blown it with *The Oracle*, too. Why had she even bothered telling Penny to trust her? Obviously no one could rely on her anymore.

And it was time for Elizabeth to do something about it!

Six

Jessica counted the bills in her wallet for the third time during study hall Friday afternoon. She couldn't stand it! School was going to let out in an hour and a half, and she was dying to go shopping to find something great to wear on her date with Charlie. But no matter how many times she counted her money, she still had only eleven dollars to her name. And even that wasn't really hers—she owed it to her mother.

Lila Fowler came over to sit next to Jessica in the lounge. "You shouldn't flash your money around, Jess. It's really tacky—and someone might try to steal your wallet," she said in her know-it-all voice.

Jessica glared at her. Trust Lila to have an

opinion about what to do with a wallet. Lila, whose father was made of money and wildly generous on top of it!

Suddenly Jessica's mood brightened. "Lila," she said in a sweet voice, "do you have any money I can borrow? Just for a week or two," she added quickly. "I'll pay you back. But I have a big date with Charlie tomorrow afternoon and nothing to wear."

Lila shook her head. "Sorry, Jess. But I have a rule. I never loan money to friends." She made it sound as though she was doing Jessica a favor. "Don't look at me that way," Lila added accusingly. "I guess you still haven't figured out the best part about your parents being separated."

"What are you talking about?" Jessica demanded.

Lila shook her head. "Look, your dad probably feels guilty about what's happened to you guys. *And* he's living all by himself, with no one to bug him for an allowance anymore. Try asking *him* for money." Lila winked. "I saw it on a soap opera once. The girl on the series had money coming out of her ears!"

Jessica didn't answer. As far as she could tell, Lila didn't know what it meant to worry about money! But she did have a point. Maybe if she just happened to drop by her father's apartment later on this evening, just to say hi, and just happen to mention she had a big date coming up and nothing to wear . . .

"Thanks," Jessica said, jumping up and stuffing her wallet back in her purse. Lila could be a pain sometimes, but she sure knew how to get things out of people!

Elizabeth closed her volume of *Othello*. She really wanted to concentrate on what Mr. Collins was saying, but she felt as if she had no energy left.

Mr. Collins cleared his throat. "OK, that pretty much sums up our study of Shakespeare's *Othello*. But I don't want you to forget the play. Try to spend some time on your own thinking about the themes we've discussed. Why does Shakespeare choose a love story to turn into a tragedy? Why can't Othello and Desdemona stay happy?"

The bell rang, and Mr. Collins gave the class a resigned smile. "And on that note, have a good weekend!" he exclaimed. School was letting out early that day because of a teachers' meeting.

Elizabeth stood up slowly, gathering her books and her jacket. She didn't know how good her weekend was going to be, but she hoped at least it would be productive. She wanted to try to rewrite her *Othello* essay and schedule a second interview with Mr. Fisherman. And she also wanted to spend as much time with her mother as she could. She was sure her mother was dreading spending the weekend by herself after so many years of marriage. The least Elizabeth could do would be to ease her loneliness by keeping her mother company.

Todd was waiting for her outside of English class, his jacket slung over one shoulder. For just an instant Elizabeth felt butterflies in her stomach, the way she had when she and Todd first met. He was so cute, with his curly brown hair and chocolate-brown eyes, and he was wearing a maroon-and-blue plaid flannel shirt she had always loved on him.

"Hey," he said, leaning over and giving her a warm hug. "Remember me? I just thought I'd come charm you to death and see if I couldn't convince you to fall in love with me all over again." His eyes were dancing.

Elizabeth couldn't help melting a little. "Todd, you're amazing," she said softly, falling into step beside him as they headed down the hall toward their lockers. "I don't know what I would have done this past couple of weeks without you. Really."

Todd grinned. "Good. That means I did the right thing buying tickets to hear Sondra Gray at the Palace tonight." The Palace was a popular music club downtown that featured vocal artists from all over the country, and Sondra Gray was one of Elizabeth's favorite singers.

For some reason, though, Elizabeth wasn't excited about the idea of going to the Palace. "Tonight?" she repeated blankly, staring at him.

"Yeah, tonight," he said, teasing her a little. "What's the matter? Do you have another date?"

Elizabeth didn't say anything for a minute. She wasn't sure herself why she was anything less than thrilled. After all, she and Todd always went out together on weekends. Sometimes going out just meant hanging around at his house or at hers, but they both saved weekend time for each other. And Elizabeth had never felt tied down by Todd, not once the whole time they had been dating. She happened to like being involved with just one boy—unlike Jessica, who never stayed with one boy for long.

So why wasn't Elizabeth glad that Todd had come up with a great plan for a Friday night together?

An image flashed through her mind then that she couldn't shake. It was of her mother, sitting all by herself in the living room, watching TV.

"Todd, listen," Elizabeth said abruptly. "I don't feel like going out tonight. I've had a long week. And to be honest, this is the first Friday since Dad moved out, and . . . well, I don't know. I just don't think it's right leaving my mom home by herself."

Todd was quiet for a minute. "OK," he said at last. "I guess I'll see if I can get a refund on the tickets. So what are you going to do, Liz? Just hang out with your mom and watch TV?" He seemed hurt and disappointed.

Elizabeth shrugged. "We'll think of something. I'm sorry, Todd," she added, "but—"

"Wait a minute," Todd said, his face brightening. "What if I can get an extra ticket? Then we could ask your mom to come with us!"

Elizabeth was starting to get annoyed. Why couldn't Todd understand that she didn't want to be pressured into a date right now? "No, thanks," she said curtly. "Mom's going to be tired. And she wouldn't enjoy the Palace anyway."

Todd stopped at his locker. "Sure," he said and shrugged. "So how about tomorrow night? Can we go see a movie or something?"

Elizabeth concentrated on watching him twirl the dial on his lock. "Todd," she said quietly, "I think I need some time to be with my family. I haven't seen my father all week. And I think Steve's coming home this weekend, so . . ."

"Liz," Todd interrupted. "I know you're going through a rough time, and believe me, I understand. I know how much you need to be with your family. But you and I need some time together, too. And the truth is, you also need some time for yourself. You can't always worry about everyone else. You have to take care of you—of us."

Elizabeth stared at him. "Listen, we should probably talk about this somewhere else," she said slowly.

But Todd was too worked up now to stop. "What scares me is that I'm not sure anymore whether you even want my support. I can't tell if you want to stay with me or not. You don't confide in me anymore. I have the feeling that you'd rather go through all this on your own. Do you want me around, Liz, or don't you?"

Elizabeth was astonished. She couldn't believe Todd was asking her this! For one brief moment a terrible, dizzying sense of pain washed over her, and she was afraid she was going to break down.

Then, even more shocking, the pain was gone. She felt completely numb. "You're right, Todd. I have been acting like a jerk," she said slowly. "I guess I've just been kidding myself. I'm too confused right now to be in a relationship. I don't even know what I want anymore."

Todd stared at her. "You can't really mean that."

Elizabeth felt perfectly calm. "You said it yourself, Todd. I'm too involved in what's going on with my family now to have enough time for you. And let's face it—I haven't been myself lately. You know what? I think I'm so scared of what's happened to my parents that I just don't feel ready to care about anyone." She cleared her throat. "Not even someone as wonderful as you."

Todd stared down at the floor. Elizabeth could see him blink away tears, and a tiny voice inside her asked if she really knew what she was doing.

But what amazed her was how calm she felt. She knew intellectually that she and Todd were talking about breaking up—about ending a relationship that had survived many changes. But she felt as though she were watching it happen from far away. She didn't even feel very moved. Besides, she knew she was doing the right thing.

Yes, she felt sorry for Todd, but she couldn't say for sure that she *loved* him. All she knew was that she was sick and tired of disappointing the people in her life.

She was actually grateful that Todd had forced her to admit her true feelings and make a clean break. They could have gone on for months together before they came to the same inevitable result.

Because in all her confusion, there was one thing that Elizabeth was very sure of: Sooner or later, every love affair ended. In fairy tales people met, fell in love, and lived happily ever after. But not in real life. In real life love ended—

sadly, disappointingly, and tragically. Shakespeare had realized that, too. That was what Elizabeth intended to say when she rewrote her essay on *Othello*. Shakespeare had written a tragedy about marriage because that's what marriage was—*tragic*.

Elizabeth had decided over the course of the past few weeks that she was never going to get married. Never. She would spend a lot of time on her writing and keep busy doing things with friends. But she was never going to get attached to one person again.

Not now that she knew what happened when you did. Not now that she was certain there was no such thing as a happy ending.

Alice Wakefield looked at Elizabeth with concern. It was Friday evening, and Elizabeth had changed into a pair of sweatpants and a T-shirt to watch the movie she and her mother had rented from the video store.

"You're sure you want to spend your Friday night doing this?" Mrs. Wakefield asked.

Elizabeth laughed. "Why not?" she said, settling down on the couch and using the remote control to turn on the TV.

She and her mother had the house to themselves. Jessica had announced, to everyone's surprise, that she was having dinner with her father downtown, and Steven wasn't coming in from college until the next morning. Elizabeth was more glad than ever that she had turned Todd down. *Mom needs me,* she thought. *I couldn't possibly leave her here alone!*

No sooner had they gotten past the credits than the telephone rang.

"I'll get it," Elizabeth volunteered, pressing the pause button. She hurried into the kitchen, where she picked up the receiver.

It was Todd.

"Liz, listen, I think we're making a big mistake," he said, before she could get a word in. "I'm serious. Do you have any idea how much you mean to me?"

Elizabeth looked with consternation at the receiver. "Todd, listen, I can't talk now. My mom and I are watching a movie. Besides, you and I went over all of this before." A note of impatience crept into her voice. Why couldn't Todd understand that this was for the best?

"Let's just get together tomorrow and talk again. In person," Todd begged.

Elizabeth didn't want to see Todd again. She didn't want to go over and over painful subjects. "Todd, I said everything I wanted to say earlier," she continued in a low voice. "We can talk at school on Monday, but not before."

She knew she sounded heartless, but she didn't intend to lead Todd on—and she didn't intend to have a lot of big melodramatic scenes, either. If the relationship was over, it was over, and that was that! "Goodbye," she said, quickly hanging up before Todd could say another word.

Mrs. Wakefield was flipping through a magazine when Elizabeth came back into the living room. She looked up at her daughter. "Who was that?" she asked.

"Todd," Elizabeth said.

"Is he OK?" Mrs. Wakefield asked.

Elizabeth nodded. "He's fine."

She felt bad lying to her mother, but there would be time enough to tell her that she and Todd had broken up. For now, Elizabeth just wanted them both to relax and enjoy the movie. Her mother had enough things to worry about without adding Elizabeth's love life to the list!

Jessica waltzed through the front door at about ten o'clock, humming to herself. She was clearly in a great mood.

"How's Daddy?" Elizabeth asked. She felt funny talking to her sister about having dinner with her father and not having been a part of it. Mrs. Wakefield had gone to bed early, and Elizabeth was watching the news on TV. She wasn't that interested, but she didn't feel like doing anything else. "How does he look?" she continued.

"He looks fine," Jessica said airily. She looked closely at her sister. "A lot better than you do, to tell you the truth. What's wrong with you? You look like you just lost your best friend."

Elizabeth sighed heavily. "Todd and I broke up today," she blurted out. She hadn't intended to tell her twin sister what had happened, but the words just slipped out.

"Really? You're kidding!" Jessica said, fascinated. "Why?"

Jessica had never been the biggest fan of her sister's relationship with Todd Wilkins. Not that she didn't think Todd was cute—and eligible enough that even *she* had been interested in him, way back in the distant past. But going with only one guy seemed like a dumb idea to her.

"I don't know. Since all this stuff's been going on with Mom and Dad, I just haven't felt good about being so serious with someone. Not now, anyway," Elizabeth said slowly.

"Good thinking," Jessica said, nodding her head. "You know what you need, Lizzie? You need to date. Ever since you started high school you've had a serious boyfriend. Why don't you try just playing the field for a while?"

Elizabeth stared at her. "You mean . . . going out with more than one boy at once?"

"Bingo!" Jessica said teasingly. "Now you've got the right idea!"

Elizabeth fiddled with the lavaliere necklace her parents had given her for her sixteenth birthday. Jessica had one just like it. Should she take her sister's advice and try to go out with as many different boys as she could? It certainly seemed to work for Jessica. And she liked the idea of not being tied down to anyone in particular.

Why not? Elizabeth thought with sudden defiance. Maybe meeting—and dating—a lot of different guys would take her mind off her troubles at home. It certainly couldn't make things worse!

Seven

Jessica twirled around in front of the mirror in her bedroom. "Great, aren't they?" she asked Amy, who was lying on Jessica's bed watching her get ready for her date with Charlie.

She was referring to the suede vest and western-looking jeans she had bought that morning at the mall. Jessica knew she looked great in whatever the latest fashion was, and this style was no exception. She could just imagine how good she would look skating around the rink, her arm linked through Charlie's . . .

"That vest must've cost a fortune," Amy observed. "Is it real suede?"

"Of course it's real," Jessica said. "My dad gave me the money," she added, fingering the material. "He thought I needed a little cheering up when I met him for dinner last night. So he told me to buy myself something special." *Just as Lila predicted*, she added to herself. Her father had seemed so guilty when Jessica said she was unhappy that he had looked as if he would give her the world!

Deep down Jessica felt a stab of guilt for manipulating her father under such lousy circumstances. But it was harmless, she assured herself. Anyway, it was only one little outfit, and she needed it. She had been building up to this date with Charlie for weeks—longer almost than she'd ever been interested in a guy before! She didn't want to take any chances on not looking her best. She would have to sneak out of the house, though. If her mother caught her wearing new clothes that her father had paid for, she would be furious!

"Remember," she said to Amy, "stay out of our way at the rink today. If you have to go there yourself to make sure Charlie really meets me, that's your problem. But I don't want you spoiling things for me." Jessica dotted some blusher along her cheekbones, then sucked in her breath to check the effect.

Amy sat up on the bed. "Guess who I ran into today on the way over here?"

Jessica fluffed up her hair. "Who?"

"Todd Wilkins. He looked like something right

out of one of those tragedies Mr. Collins has been making us read," Amy added with a giggle. "Before I could even ask him what was wrong, he told me that Elizabeth broke up with him!"

"I know," Jessica said calmly. "My sister happens to have seen the light, and she doesn't feel like being tied down anymore."

Amy's eyes narrowed. "Really? Well, all I know is that he looked so sad. . . ." She thought for a moment. "Actually, he looked even cuter than he usually does." She sat up on the bed. "What do you think, Jess? Can you see Todd and me together—as a couple?"

"A couple of whats?" Jessica replied sarcastically. Before Amy could say another word, Jessica cut her off. "Don't even think about it, Amy. Todd and Liz may have split up for a while, but that doesn't mean *you* can have him. Liz would be furious with you, which means I'd have to be mad at you, too."

Amy shrugged. "Yeah, well, you know what they say: 'All's fair in love and war.' I mean, if Liz dropped him, then he's fair game as far as I'm concerned." She tossed back her straight blond hair. "You never know, Jess. Todd and I might be destined for each other."

Jessica groaned. "Listen, I don't want to be late. I told Charlie I'd meet him at the rink in fifteen minutes." She gave her hair one last furious brushstroke and then decided she shouldn't tamper with perfection.

Amy doesn't know anything about destiny, she thought. *Charlie and I, however, were made for each other—I can tell!*

The roller rink was crowded with the usual Saturday afternoon assortment of little kids, parents, and couples skating in pairs. Jessica nervously ran her fingers through her hair as she glanced up at the huge clock on the far wall of the rink. It was three o'clock. Where was Charlie?

She scanned the bleachers, then the concession stand and the benches where people were changing into skates—still no Charlie. Jessica had already put her skates on. She did an experimental turn on the wooden floor and was just about to spin into a figure eight when a little boy crashed into her, knocking her down.

"Ow!" Jessica said, rubbing her knee.

Just then a boy skated up, a look of concern on his face. "Are you all right?" he asked, holding out his hand to help her up.

Jessica glared at him. "I'm fine. Don't worry—I can get up myself," she muttered.

Then she saw the red rose in his other hand.

"Omigosh. Are you . . . you must be Charlie," she said, blushing right to the roots of her hair. "I'm Jessica."

He nodded. "Hi," he said stiffly. His voice sounded a little different in person than it had on the phone, higher or something. *Well, maybe I sound different, too,* Jessica thought.

As she struggled to her feet, Jessica tried to get a good look at him without being too obvious. He was tall—about six feet two—with fairly thick sandy blond hair. His face was classically handsome, almost *too* handsome, with chiseled features and very smooth skin. He had dark eyes and a perfect smile, and he was dressed in clothes that Jessica definitely approved of: jeans and a trendy sweater. So why did she feel strangely disappointed?

"Are you hurt?" Charlie asked, still looking concerned.

"Nah. That kid just doesn't know a professional skater when he sees one," Jessica said, laughing.

Charlie didn't laugh with her. He just stood there, awkwardly holding the rose in his hand.

"Oh!" he said suddenly, as if remembering. "This is for you." He handed the rose to her and smiled.

"Thanks," Jessica said. She couldn't help noticing that Charlie's smile was forced. "But I don't think it's going to do any better on the rink than I did. Can we leave it over with our coats?"

"Better on the rink than you did?" Charlie repeated uncomprehendingly.

Jessica coughed. "Never mind. I'll put it over here," she said quickly. Once she was at the side of the rink, she turned and checked out Charlie from a distance. He was very good-looking, there was no doubt about it. But as far as personality went, Charlie seemed to be made out of cardboard. Where was the warm, witty guy she'd gotten to know over the phone?

She skated back to join him, and he smiled his plastic smile at her again.

"Do you like to roller-skate, Jessica?" he asked eagerly.

Jessica tried to hide a smile. *What a great conversationalist!* she thought. *What's he going to do next—talk about the weather?*

"Roller-skating's OK. It's safer than skydiving, anyway," she said, doing a few spins.

Charlie's eyes widened. "You've been skydiving?" he repeated incredulously.

"No—I was just kidding," Jessica said with a faint laugh.

Here she had been telling everyone what a great sense of humor Charlie had and how romantic he was. And now that they'd finally met, she was finding out just the opposite. He hadn't responded to her jokes, and he didn't seem at all interested in holding her hand as they skated around the rink.

"Gee, you skate well," he said, after a few laps.

Jessica sighed. This was getting worse by the minute. "Listen, Charlie," she said, "you sound different today than you usually do on the phone. You're not nervous about meeting me in person, are you?" she demanded.

Charlie wet his lip. "Uh—no, Jessica. See, my voice changes in different circumstances," he added quickly.

Great, Jessica thought. *What does that mean?*

"Excuse me," Charlie said a minute later, "but do you see that blond girl over there? Do you know her?"

Jessica decided to avoid that question by changing the subject. She tucked her arm through Charlie's. "Come on—let's try to speed things up a little. Can't you skate any faster?"

Charlie blushed a deep crimson. "You're too good for me," he said sadly.

Jessica took his hand in hers, a decision she regretted at once. His palm was clammy.

"Just try pushing a little harder with each step," she suggested kindly.

Amy winked at her across the floor, and Jessica had to hide her fury. This was *not* working out the way she had planned. Charlie was a lot of fun on the phone, but in person he was a big disappointment. Good-looking, yes, but a disappointment nonetheless. She could hardly wait till her "mystery date" was over!

"Jessica! Telephone for you!" Elizabeth called upstairs on Saturday evening.

Jessica picked up the receiver in her bedroom, not even bothering to close the romance novel she was reading.

"Hello?" she said in a bored voice.

"You, Jessica, are the most dazzling, the most wonderful, and the wittiest roller-skater known to man. Or to woman, for that matter. Do you know I've been thinking about you ever since we said goodbye at the rink?"

Jessica couldn't believe her ears. "Charlie?" she said.

"I miss you," he said in a soft voice. "Jessica, when you touched my hand this afternoon . . . do you know I was struck positively dumb?"

Jessica frowned. "It did seem to take you by surprise," she said slowly. "Charlie, were you feeling all right this afternoon? You didn't seem like yourself."

"I was a little shy," Charlie admitted. "I had no idea you'd be as beautiful as you are. I mean . . . well, after all these phone calls, I couldn't help thinking that maybe I was expecting too much. Then I saw you—and that was it, Jess.

Instant love." He sighed. "How could you expect me not to be tongue-tied?"

Jessica didn't know what to think. "I was kind of confused—" she began.

"Listen," he said urgently, cutting her off. "I need another chance. Will you have dinner with me one night this week? How about Wednesday?"

Jessica thought for a minute. "I guess that would be all right," she said, still feeling confused about what had happened at the rink.

"Terrific! I can't wait to see you again!"

This is so weird, Jessica thought after she and Charlie had said goodbye. Talk about split personalities! That afternoon, Charlie had seemed so shy and awkward, she couldn't think of a single thing to say to him. But tonight he was back to his old self—confident, clever, and romantic.

Maybe he just doesn't do well on first dates, she thought philosophically. *After all, he did say he was bowled over by my* pretty *face!* Jessica wouldn't mind giving him a second chance. Date number two with Charlie Ryan was going to be a night to remember!

Elizabeth was reading the Sunday paper out by the pool the next day when Enid dropped by.

"I wanted to return these," she said, tossing a couple of paperbacks onto the deck chair next to Elizabeth.

"Thanks," Elizabeth said, giving her friend a smile. "Do you want some orange juice or soda or something?"

Enid pulled up a chair and sat down. "Actually, what I really want is to talk to you. I ran into Todd yesterday. Liz, what's going on between you two?"

Elizabeth bit her lip. "Enid, it just isn't working out. I don't know what to tell you. I don't feel I can talk about it right now."

"It hurts too much, right?" Enid's green eyes were compassionate. "Look, Liz, I know that your parents' separation is probably the toughest thing you've ever had to deal with. And believe me, I know how lonesome and confusing a time this can be! But you can't shut out your friends, Liz. Not me—and not Todd."

Elizabeth stared at the paper in her lap. "Todd doesn't want to be friends, Enid. He wants more from me. And I'm not ready for that right now. I don't know if I'll ever be," she explained.

Enid was shocked by Elizabeth's words. "He said you wouldn't even meet him to talk about it," she protested.

Elizabeth picked up her glass of juice and took a sip. Deep inside she still felt numb about everything that was happening with her and Todd. She couldn't even remember why they had become a couple in the first place. "Look, I said I can't talk about it, and I mean that. Honestly, Enid. It's all for the best. I'd only hurt Todd in the long run, anyway—or he'd hurt me."

From the look on Enid's face, Elizabeth could tell she was disappointing her best friend. Enid obviously wanted her and Todd to get back together. But what was the point?

The truth was, she was glad things were over with Todd. Her talk with Jessica had convinced her that it was stupid to get tied to one guy. She didn't want to get all wrapped up in someone else's life. She would only end up ruining the relationship or getting hurt—or both.

No, the new Elizabeth Wakefield was going to play the field and enjoy it!

Eight

Elizabeth tugged her skirt hem self-consciously. "Well, here goes nothing," she murmured. It was Monday morning, and she was in the girls' bathroom nearest to her locker, looking uneasily at the outfit she had chosen for her first day back in public as a single girl. The denim miniskirt looked more like something Jessica would wear. "But I want to be more like Jessica," Elizabeth reminded herself.

She took a deep breath and practiced a flirtatious smile in the mirror. *Not bad*, she praised herself. *Not bad at all.*

In fact, she kept the smile on her face as she walked out into the hallway—and smack into Todd.

"Liz!" he cried, overjoyed to see her. His glance took in everything, her miniskirt, her fluffed-up hair.

But the smile on her face vanished the minute she saw him. "Oh—hi, Todd," she said casually.

"You know, I called you this morning to see if you wanted a ride. But your mom told me you'd already gone," he said, falling into step beside her.

Elizabeth didn't know what to say. It made her feel really uncomfortable to see how much Todd still wanted to be with her. *Forget about me, Todd*, she warned him silently. *You don't want to go out with someone like me.*

Todd was uncharacteristically quiet, too. He seemed to want to say more, but he didn't.

"Listen, I have to run," Elizabeth told him as they turned the corner. "I promised Penny I'd meet with her before homeroom. Can we catch up later on?"

"Sure," Todd said, shrugging his shoulders. He was acting nonchalant, but his brown eyes betrayed his sadness. Elizabeth could feel him watching her as she bounded off down the hall. She hoped he would get over it soon, so they could both get on with their lives!

"Liz? Is that you?" Enid demanded, setting her lunch tray down next to her friend. "I thought you were Jessica. Since when do you wear a skirt the size of a Band-Aid to school?"

Elizabeth took a bite of her salad. "Since today," she said calmly.

"Liz, I overheard Paul Jeffries in the lunch line. He was bragging that he has a date with you tonight!" Enid looked at her in disbelief. "He was lying, wasn't he?"

Elizabeth shook her head. "He asked me to go to the movies with him, and I said sure. Why not?" she asked. "There's nothing wrong with going out with someone new."

As a matter of fact, Elizabeth was more than a little proud of her conquest. Paul was a cute senior who had written a few articles for *The Oracle*, and she thought he had real possibilities. He was tall, with dark curly hair, a nice smile, and a great personality. He had only recently broken up with his girlfriend, and a lot of people thought he was the most eligible guy at school.

"Well, there's nothing wrong with it," Enid said, "except that Paul happens to be a real womanizer. He's gone out with about a dozen girls this month alone. You'd better watch out, Liz."

Elizabeth dabbed her mouth with a napkin. "I'll be fine, Enid. I appreciate your looking out for me, but don't worry."

Enid leaned forward across the table. "You

may get mad at me for saying this, but Todd's been bugging me about you nonstop. He really misses you, and he feels like you two made a mistake splitting up. He needs to talk to you. Can't you give him one more chance?"

Elizabeth sighed. "Enid, I can't say this to Todd, but I can at least tell *you* the truth. I just don't feel it was a mistake. I don't feel anything, to be honest. Maybe relieved, but not upset."

Enid shrugged. "Well, I still can't see why you'd want to waste your time with someone like Paul when you could be with Todd," she muttered. "But I guess it isn't any of my business."

Elizabeth didn't answer. How could she explain to Enid that what she wanted right now was just to have fun? Of course she knew that Paul wouldn't be right for the long term. But that was one of the things that made him appealing to her.

She didn't believe in long term anymore. And even more to the point, Elizabeth knew she didn't deserve a boyfriend like Todd. Not the way she had been messing things up lately.

Jessica twirled her "Wakefield for Mayor" button as she looked around the crowded restaurant. It was Wednesday night, and she was supposed to be meeting Charlie for dinner, but he was nowhere in sight. The fact that he'd been late for both dates didn't exactly win him any points with her—she was used to guys waiting for *her*!

A waiter passed her carrying a large tray of plates filled with sushi. Jessica swallowed nervously. Charlie was the one who had suggested Japanese food, and Jessica, wanting to be a good sport, had said that was fine. Now she wondered if she was crazy. Could she really eat raw fish?

Charlie Ryan, you'd better be worth all this, she thought.

She shifted from one foot to the other, trying to catch a glimpse of herself in the mirror across the room. It had been a weird week, and Jessica wasn't sure if she was really in the mood for this second try with Charlie. Things at home had been really strange, she thought. Something had really come over Elizabeth, for one thing! At first Jessica had been pleased to hear that Elizabeth and Todd had broken up. But she hadn't expected her twin to undergo a personality change! In the last three days, Elizabeth had gone out with two different guys: Paul Jeffries on Monday, and Steve Anderson, a quiet but attractive junior, on Tuesday. That was moving a little fast, even in Jessica's opinion.

Jessica was a little worried about her sister.

But Elizabeth hadn't been very easy to talk to lately.

"It's all for the best," was all she would say.

"Does that mean you don't even care that Amy Sutton wants to make a try for Todd?" Jessica had asked her innocently, earlier.

For a second—just one—she thought she had gotten a rise out of her sister, who turned a little pale. But all Elizabeth said, in a flat, super-controlled voice, was, "If Todd wants to go out with Amy, he's welcome to. It's a free country."

Jessica sighed now, as she looked at her watch. Where was Charlie, anyway? She didn't like being kept waiting!

The door of the restaurant opened, and in he came, looking even more handsome this time in a leather jacket, denim shirt, and gray trousers.

"Hi," he said somewhat stiffly.

"Hi," Jessica said coolly, tapping her foot against the carpet. Wasn't he going to at least kiss her on the cheek?

"Oh—here," he said, awkwardly thrusting another rose at her.

One of the thorns scratched Jessica's hand. "Ouch!" Jessica said, checking to see if he had drawn blood.

Charlie didn't even notice. "Let's sit down," he said. "I'm starving."

Jessica gulped as she caught another glimpse

of the raw fish. She wasn't *that* hungry. Something told her she was in for a long evening.

Charlie was certainly polite, she had to give him that. He ushered her over to the table, waited until she sat down to push in her chair, and he was so careful about shaking out his napkin and spreading it on his lap that Jessica had to suppress her laughter.

The problem was, he just didn't have any personality—or a sense of humor. She decided to keep trying, though. After all, he was hilarious on the phone. *Maybe he's still nervous*, she thought. "Hey," she said with a giggle, covering her mouth. "Look at that woman over there. She's obviously regretting *that* order!"

Charlie turned to regard the tiny woman, who was struggling to eat a mountain of tempura. But he didn't even smile as he turned back. He just looked seriously at Jessica. "She doesn't look worried to me."

Jessica sighed. "Never mind. Let's order."

Reading the menu didn't exactly lift her spirits. Jessica knew famous models swore by sushi, since it was nutritious and low in calories. But at the moment all she wanted was a hamburger or pizza—something American. Nothing on the menu sounded good to her.

"Hey," she said as she read the menu, "isn't there some kind of raw fish that can kill you with a single taste?"

Charlie raised his eyebrows. "I don't think so," he said. "I guess you could get sick if it was spoiled, though."

Jessica set down the menu and stared at the clock on the wall. It was only seven o'clock. *Move*, she silently ordered the hands. *Move!*

"Jessica, thank you for dinner. That was so nice," Charlie said an hour and a half later. They were on the stoop in front of the Wakefields' front door. Although Jessica had driven to the restaurant, Charlie had insisted on following her home in his car.

Jessica tried to smile. *Please don't try to kiss me*, she was thinking. "Yes, it *was* nice," she lied.

She shouldn't have worried about Charlie making a pass at her. She had never seen a guy so awkward as he was just then! He was practically wringing his hands, he was so nervous. Finally he blurted out, "Can I see you again?"

Jessica took a deep breath. This wasn't a position she really liked to be in. Even though Elizabeth sometimes accused her of being heartless, she hated turning guys down. But two dates with Charlie had been enough to convince her that he wasn't the guy for her. True, on the phone he was incredibly fun. He had a wonderful personality, a sparkling sense of humor, and managed to make half of what he said sound like poetry. But something happened to him in person, and he turned into a giant dud.

Maybe that's why he was drawn to the phone line, Jessica thought.

"Listen, Charlie, I have to be honest with you. I don't think we should see each other again. I don't think we're right for each other," she said hurriedly.

"You don't?" he repeated blankly. "But I thought—"

"I like you and everything, you're a nice guy, but . . ." Jessica shrugged. "It just isn't there, Charlie." She gave him her sweetest smile. "But we can still be friends. And we can still talk on the phone. Only not on the party line. It costs too much."

"You're sure you won't go out with me—not even one more time?"

"I'm sure, Charlie. But thanks, anyway," Jessica said politely.

She was positive she had done the right thing. It wasn't easy to give up her romantic fantasy of Charlie Ryan. But now that she'd met him, it just wasn't the same. There was no spark between them, and Jessica wasn't going to pretend —not even for another date—that there was.

"So it didn't work out with you and Mr. Telephone Man, huh?" Amy joked the next day. Amy and Jessica were sitting outside on the lawn after school, relaxing for a few minutes before cheerleading practice.

"He was totally different in person than he was on the phone. And the difference *didn't* work in his favor," Jessica said.

Amy raised her eyebrows. "It's not as if he wasn't cute, Jess—at least from the glimpse I got at the roller-skating rink."

Jessica shrugged. "To tell you the truth, I would've liked it better if he was a little less good-looking and had a little more personality."

Amy giggled. "Yeah, I bet. You've never gone out *once* with a guy who wasn't cute."

"That's a rotten thing to say," Jessica snapped. "I just happen to go out with guys I like. If I ever like a guy who isn't cute, I'll go out with him."

Amy raised one eyebrow. "You mean to say that if this guy Charlie had been every bit as wonderful in person as he was on the phone, and just *happened* to be a little weird looking, that you'd have gone out with him?"

"Of course!" Jessica replied. She didn't like the skeptical expression on her friend's face. Amy was one to talk—she only went out with the most gorgeous guys at school!

Jessica was about to remind her of that when Paul Jeffries came bounding across the lawn. Jessica didn't know Paul very well, but she had always admired him from a distance.

"Hey," he said, "I've been looking all over for you!"

Jessica's spirits lifted right away. She knew she wouldn't have to wait long before someone better than Charlie came along!

"You have?" she repeated in her most flirtatious voice.

Paul blinked. "Whoops," he said, turning a little bit red. "I can't believe I just did that. I thought you were Liz," he added.

Jessica couldn't believe her ears. "Liz?" she repeated incredulously.

"She and I were supposed to go get some ice cream, and when I saw you out here . . ." Paul shrugged, his gray-blue eyes twinkling. "This must happen to you all the time. I'd better go. See you later." And before Jessica could tell him how rude he was, he took off.

"Well, well, well," Amy said, getting to her feet. "That's kind of a switch, isn't it? Your sister's really been getting around this week. That's her second date with Paul Jeffries, and I saw her playing tennis with that guy Steve from our math class. I think Lila saw her at the beach yesterday with the new junior from Texas, John Campbell. You know who I mean—the really cute guy with red hair and those wonderful green eyes?"

"So what?" Jessica snapped. "Elizabeth can do what she wants. It's no big deal."

"Well, I just thought, you know, that maybe

it was starting to bug you . . . seeing your sister get so much attention and all," Amy said coyly.

"Well, it isn't," Jessica retorted.

She wasn't about to admit to Amy just how much Elizabeth's behavior bothered her. The truth was, she was furious with Elizabeth for showing her up at school. She was acting like a selfish, spoiled brat, going out with all the best-looking guys as if she were trying to prove something. Maybe she was, but Jessica thought Elizabeth was carrying things a little too far. And she intended to tell her so!

Nine

Jessica's mood got worse and worse that Thursday afternoon. First, she ran out of gas four blocks from home and had to walk almost a mile to the gas station and beg someone to drive her back and fill the tank for her. Then, when she finally got home, she realized she'd forgotten her house keys, and no one was home.

What a family, she thought angrily, sitting down on the front stoop. Her mother was off working until all hours of the night, instead of waiting for her at home the way moms on TV did. Her brother had been acting like a total and complete jerk ever since their parents' separation. Their poor father had been driven away and now lived in a dingy little apartment all by himself. She sniffed sadly. On top of everything else, Elizabeth was getting a reputation that wasn't exactly flattering—and she was stealing all of Jessica's potential boyfriends!

A few clouds rolled over the sun, and Jessica heaved a loud sigh. "Great," she muttered. "It'll probably rain on me next."

She was just getting ready for a good long sulk when she heard the sound of a car turning into the driveway. She looked up, hoping it was her mother.

But to her disgust it was Steven's yellow Volkswagen.

"What are *you* doing here?" she said in an accusing voice, forgetting to be glad about the fact that Steven would have a key. "This is getting ridiculous. You've been here practically every night lately."

"What a nice thing to say," Steven said sarcastically. He got out of the car and picked up his textbooks from the passenger's seat. "I don't suppose you care about the fact that I'm trying to be around more since Mom and Dad split up."

"Yeah," Jessica muttered, her arms crossed defensively over her chest. "I'm sure you really think you can do a lot of good." She glared at him. "You haven't even asked *once* about Daddy's campaign for mayor. All you care about is supporting Mom."

Steven shot her an annoyed look. "If you really want to know the truth, Jess, I think Dad's campaign for mayor is more than a little half-baked. I know he got roped into it by Mr. Patman and that political consultant friend of his, but I don't think he has much of a chance. He doesn't have any experience in public service. He's a good lawyer—a great lawyer—but not a mayor." He walked up to the stoop and set down his books. "But that doesn't mean I don't support Dad for trying, Jess. It's just—"

"It's just that he doesn't spoil you rotten the way Mom does," Jessica said.

"Jessica, you're really starting to make me mad," Steven said in a cold voice. "And incidentally, what are you doing hanging around outside? Don't you have anything better to do than pick fights with me? I would've thought you'd have cheerleading or a sorority meeting or one of those other really pressing commitments of yours."

Jessica glared at him. "I forgot my keys," she muttered.

She wasn't enjoying this one bit. And the situation got even worse when Elizabeth came coasting up on her bike a minute later.

"Steve!" she cried, as if a visit from her brother was the most exciting thing in the world.

She barely even said hello to Jessica. Not that Jessica would have wanted her to be friendly, the way she was feeling toward her.

"Where have you been, Liz?" Jessica demanded. "Out with someone new? Or have you decided to take it easy and just have four dates this week?"

Elizabeth looked stunned. "Wh-what?" she choked out.

Steven was surprised, too. "Isn't that kind of out of line, Jessica—even for you?"

"I was at Enid's," Elizabeth added. A strained silence hung in the air as she and Jessica stared at each other.

"Well, all I know is that everyone's been talking about you at school," Jessica said. "It's one thing being on the rebound and going out on a date or two. You've seen three different guys in the same week! People think . . . well, *you know*." She gave her sister a knowing look. "Maybe you should take it easy."

"You're the one who told me to play the field in the first place!" Elizabeth argued.

"Playing the field is one thing. Going for all the players at the same time is another," Jessica said hotly.

Steven looked astonished. "What happened to Todd?" he asked.

Elizabeth turned beet red. "Todd and I broke up," she told her brother, "and the truth is, I *have* been spending time with a few different friends who happen to be guys—but it's no one's business. And it's hardly the way you're making it seem, Jessica," she added defensively.

Jessica shrugged. "I'm not the one who's making it seem that way. The facts speak for themselves." She knew she was being mean, but she was still stinging from her run-in with Paul Jeffries. Jessica hated being humiliated, and right now she felt so frustrated—and so confused—that she couldn't help striking out at her brother and sister.

Elizabeth took a deep breath. "Can we at least all go inside? I'm dying of thirst, and I need something cold to drink."

Jessica shrugged as Steven unlocked the door. She knew her sister well enough to guess Elizabeth was trying to change the subject.

"Even Amy Sutton thinks you've gone overboard," she told Elizabeth in the front hallway.

Elizabeth just ignored her. "Steve, how did you manage to make it home again? It's so great to see you!" she said. Her voice was quivering a little, and Jessica knew she was trying to act as if everything were fine.

"He came home to take care of Mom," Jessica informed her twin. "Didn't you, Steve? But he's forgotten that he ever had a father. Ask him the last time he talked to Dad—even on the phone," she added tauntingly.

Steven walked up to Jessica and looked her right in the eye. "I've taken just about enough of this from you. If you say one more time that I haven't been in touch with Dad—"

"You haven't! You're lying if you say you have!" Jessica shrieked.

Elizabeth's gaze flashed from one to the other. "Stop it, you two!" she begged. "Listen, you guys are both upset about the same thing, even though you keep fighting about it. Steve, you're as sad as Jess is about Mom and Dad splitting up. You don't really love Mom any more than you love Dad. It's just that somehow—and I don't really understand how—you've taken her side, and Jessica, you've taken Dad's side, and now the two of you are mad at each other when there's no need to be!"

Jessica didn't think she could stand another second of this. "And you're the perfect one, I suppose," she said acidly. "Why should this time be any different from usual? I'm impulsive and Steven's stubborn and only Elizabeth is perfectly reasonable." She glared at her sister. "Why don't you stop and listen to yourself for once? You sound so self-satisfied!"

"That's a really rude thing to say, Jess," Steven said. "You owe Liz an apology."

"I do not. I'm sick and tired of Liz acting like she's so perfect all the time!"

"I don't act that way," Elizabeth protested.

"You do so!" Jessica cried.

"Quit it, the two of you!" Steven said, throwing up his hands in exasperation. "Can't you act your age? You're sixteen, not six."

"Steve—" Elizabeth began.

"I'm not kidding," Steven interrupted. "I'm sick of you two squabbling. I wouldn't have to keep coming home so much if I believed you two could get along with each other and help Mom out."

"Oh, and we don't help Mom? Now who's sounding like Mr. Perfect?" Jessica demanded, enraged. "Where do you think you get off, Steven?"

The anger in the room was mounting unbearably. But instead of feeling upset, Jessica was almost glad. It felt good to finally express what she had been thinking!

"It's the two of you who are both acting like six-year-olds," Elizabeth snapped. "Steve, you jump all over Jess—and, Jess, you do the same to him. Can't we at least try to pretend to be a family, since we're all we have left?"

Jessica turned to her brother. "See? There she goes again! I can't stand it. You'd think she never made a mistake in her whole life!"

"I may have made mistakes," Elizabeth began uncertainly, "but—"

"But not big ones," Jessica finished for her, mockingly. She turned back to her brother. "See what I mean?"

"Jessica's right, Liz," Steven agreed, shaking his head. "You shouldn't sound so self-righteous."

"Who's sounding self-righteous?" Elizabeth wailed.

"You are!" Steven and Jessica said in unison.

Elizabeth's face turned red with anger. "Cut it out," she muttered. "I don't want to hear another accusation!"

"No one's accusing you," Jessica said. "In fact, we've been covering up your mistakes for weeks! No one ever mentions the fact that *you're* the one who gave our phone number at Lake Tahoe to Mom's assistant. You're the one who wrecked the weekend for all of us. If it weren't for you, Mom and Dad would probably still be together!"

Shocked silence filled the air. For a minute no one said anything.

Steven turned to Elizabeth, a puzzled frown on his face. "Did you really do that?" he asked. "Why would you have given the phone number to Julia? Didn't Mom and Dad say they didn't want to be disturbed?"

Elizabeth paled. "I didn't . . . I mean, I had no idea . . ."

"You just didn't think," Jessica snapped. "And it's thoughtless acts like that one that can destroy a family."

Steven was still staring at Elizabeth. "Well," he said uncomfortably, "I'm sure that that wasn't such a big factor, Jess. Mom and Dad didn't split up because of that weekend. It isn't fair to make Liz feel rotten about it."

"But that's my point. Nobody makes her feel rotten about it. Everyone acts like it didn't even matter, when the truth is, it did. Look at poor Daddy. Here he'd gone to all that trouble to make sure the weekend was as great as it had always been, and Mom got dragged away practically as soon as we arrived." Jessica glared at her sister. "All because of you," she spat.

Elizabeth shuddered. "It wasn't my fault!" she choked out. "I didn't know that anyone from the office would actually call! And I had no idea Mom would have to leave early!"

"Sure," Jessica said and shrugged. "Tell yourself whatever you want. But look what happened. Mom left Tahoe, and she and Dad decided to split up." She snapped her fingers. "Just like that . . . the whole marriage was over. So don't go acting so perfect, Liz. You're the one who's to blame for this whole stupid mess!"

Jessica hadn't realized it, but during the fight she had been getting closer and closer to tears. Suddenly she burst out crying. She couldn't stop herself. She had finally said everything she wanted to say.

Steven looked from one twin to the other. "I don't even know what to say," he whispered.

"She's ruined everything," Jessica gasped as her brother put his arm around her shoulder to comfort her.

Neither of them even noticed when a few seconds later Elizabeth turned and fled.

*   *   *

Elizabeth sat at her desk and tried to take a deep breath to calm herself. She couldn't believe this was happening, that her worst nightmare was coming true.

Yes, she had felt guilty about that idiotic slip of hers. For weeks she'd been tormenting herself, second-guessing her decision, wishing she had never given the phone number to Julia.

At the same time, a little voice inside her had insisted that she couldn't have singlehandedly caused her parents to split up. That same voice tried to persuade her that her mistake, big as it might seem to her, wasn't really the end of the world. After all, she had confessed to her mother that she was the one who'd given the inn's phone number to Julia. And her mother hadn't been particularly upset.

But Jessica and Steven had just made the truth perfectly clear. Obviously, they had only been trying to hide it from her. Jessica had said it in anger, but she'd meant it. Elizabeth was sure of that.

It's my fault—all my fault, she told herself. Elizabeth looked around her cheerful room. *I don't deserve this*, she thought. *I don't deserve to live in this house. Not after what I've done.*

She took another deep breath, trying to calm herself, but it was impossible. Tears racked her body, and sobbing, she flung herself down on her bed.

*   *   *

"Hi, everybody!" Mrs. Wakefield called, stepping into the kitchen at six thirty-five that evening.

Jessica looked up from setting the table. "Hi, Mom," she said with a sweet smile.

"What a nice thing to do, Jess," her mother praised her. She set a bag of groceries down on the kitchen counter. "Where's Liz?"

"Upstairs, I guess," Jessica said innocently. "Steve's here," she added. She could hardly believe that she hadn't been glad to see her big brother just an hour ago. Now that he had stopped automatically defending Elizabeth, he was a lot more pleasant to be around.

"How was your day?" she asked her mother in the same sweet voice.

"Pretty good. I met your father downtown for lunch," Mrs. Wakefield said, putting the groceries away.

Jessica couldn't believe her ears. "Really? What happened? What was it like?"

Mrs. Wakefield laughed. "Hey, slow down a little. It was nice. We agreed when your father moved out that he and I would get together periodically, so we could talk about family things. Like you and Liz and Steve. And, after all," she added, "we miss each other's company. It was nice, catching up."

Jessica watched her mother warily as she finished setting the table. What did that mean that they "missed each other's company"? Were they going to start having lunch dates all the time? Did it mean they were going to make up and that her father would come home again?

All of a sudden Jessica felt a pang of longing for her father and for the way life used to be in the Wakefield house. And at the same moment she felt guilty about Elizabeth.

Maybe she shouldn't have accused her of causing the separation, she thought. It wasn't *all* Elizabeth's fault that her parents had split up. Maybe only partly—like fifty or sixty percent or so.

But Jessica wasn't good at apologizing, and she didn't feel like letting her sister off the hook that easily. And when Elizabeth excused herself from the dinner table early, claiming she wasn't very hungry, Jessica only felt the tiniest twinge of guilt. *Elizabeth will get over it*, she thought as she dug into a wedge of chocolate cake. *Besides, she has to learn that she can't go out with every boy at Sweet Valley High!*

Ten

Elizabeth drew doodles in the upper corner of her English exam on Friday afternoon. She had read the question several times: "In many of the works we've read this semester, the authors describe love as particularly fragile. Do you agree or not? Be sure to back up your claims with examples from the literature we've studied."

Elizabeth chewed on the end of her pen and stared out the window. Outside, the sky was a brilliant blue, the sun was shining, and everything looked as wonderful as it always did in Sweet Valley. Elizabeth wished her mood were *half* as sunny as it was outside.

She knew she was going to let Mr. Collins down—again. But she couldn't bring herself to recite all the reasons why great authors believed love was fragile. Elizabeth herself believed it so strongly and so painfully that her eyes filled with tears every time she started thinking about it. But she could hardly pour her heart out onto her exam paper. This just wasn't a topic she could discuss on an intellectual level.

The night before had been a completely sleepless one for Elizabeth. She had tried to sleep, knowing that exhaustion wasn't going to help anything. But every time she closed her eyes, she saw her sister's and her brother's accusing faces.

Her parents' separation was all her fault; that was the one thought that kept echoing in her mind throughout the night.

In fact, while she had lain there in bed, waiting for the sun to rise, Elizabeth had come up with hundreds of other things she'd done in the past six months or so to jeopardize her parents' relationship. Hadn't she been the one who had praised her mother so much for throwing herself into her career? And hadn't she been particularly thrilled when her mother had the opportunity to head up the design project for the new wing of the mall? There were other things, too. Little gestures she'd made, things she'd said that she would give anything now to take back.

But it was too late. Her parents' marriage was over, and it was all because of her.

The bell rang, and Elizabeth looked down with horror at her blank exam. She couldn't hand in a blank piece of paper! Blinking back tears, Elizabeth crumpled the sheet in her hand and got to her feet.

She just wouldn't hand in the test. It didn't matter, anyway. By the time Mr. Collins figured out she hadn't written the exam, she intended to be far away from Sweet Valley, somewhere where she couldn't ruin her friends' and her family's lives anymore.

"What do you mean you're leaving?" Enid demanded, her eyes wide with shock.

It was Friday after school, and the two girls were at the Box Tree Café, where Elizabeth had begged her friend to meet her.

"Just what I said—I'm leaving," Elizabeth repeated calmly. She brushed her hair back from her forehead. "Listen, Enid, I've given this a lot of thought. Believe me, I was up all night torturing myself about it. I just can't stay at home right now. It's too horrible, knowing that I—" Her voice broke. "That I caused all the problems between my mother and father. I just need to get out of here for a while." She took a deep breath. "Maybe if I leave, they'll get back together again."

"Liz, I'm sorry, but that's just ridiculous!"

Enid cried. She grabbed her friend's arm. "I've known you for a long time, and I'm not surprised that you're taking your parents' separation so hard. Most kids feel really guilty when their parents split up, and you're—well, you're pretty sensitive." Enid gave Elizabeth a pleading look. "But you're *wrong*, Liz. You have nothing to do with their decision to live apart for a while. Don't you realize that?"

"Then why did Jessica say what she did?" Elizabeth cried. "Forget it, Enid. I realize you're trying to make me feel better, but I know I'm right. I really need to get away."

Enid stared at the duffel bag under the table. "Where are you planning to go? You can't just take off, Liz. You have to have some sort of a plan."

Elizabeth fidgeted with her napkin. "I've been thinking about that," she said slowly, "and I have two ideas. The first is to go stay with my aunt and uncle and my cousin Jenny in Dallas. And if they don't feel comfortable with that, I'll call my grandparents in Michigan." She glanced up at Enid defiantly. "I know they'll let me come stay with them—at least until things smooth over."

Enid looked horrified. "You can't leave Sweet Valley! Have you thought about how your parents will feel? And Jess and Steve?"

"They wouldn't miss me," Elizabeth said sadly. "They'd be glad I was gone."

"That isn't true, Liz! And what about your friends? What about me—and Todd?"

What about Todd? Elizabeth thought. *I caused that split, too.* She took a deep breath to keep herself from breaking down. "All I know is, I can't go home right now," she managed to say.

"Well, why don't you come home with me?" Enid said briskly.

Elizabeth stared at her. "What?"

"Just what I said. Come stay at my house for a while. My mom should be understanding about this. She went through a divorce herself, remember?"

"Enid . . ." Elizabeth began, not sure what she should do.

"It may not be as exotic as running off to Texas or Michigan, but it's a lot easier. And a lot more practical," Enid added. "You can just tell your folks you want to spend a little time over at my house. They'll be calmer, too, knowing you're just around the corner."

A tear trickled down Elizabeth's face. She didn't deserve such a good friend. "You're the most wonderful friend in the whole world," she told Enid. "I can't believe you'll really let me come stay with you!"

Enid gave her a smile that was both fond and impatient. "Listen, you're going to snap out of this crazy mood of yours any minute. And for your sake, I'd rather have you right in my own house, not halfway across the country, when you finally come to your senses. Now, let's go!"

"I don't know, Enid," Elizabeth said later that afternoon. "You're sure I should send a letter to my dad as well as my mom? Won't he panic when he finds out I moved out of the house?"

"You have to let them both know. It isn't fair to tell one and not the other," Enid said judiciously.

They were up in Enid's bedroom, using her computer to compose a letter explaining what Elizabeth was doing, and why.

It was much harder than Elizabeth had thought it would be. She wrote several different versions and finally decided the simplest—and shortest—would be best.

> Dear Mom, Dad, Jessica, and Steven:
>
> I want you to know how sorry I am for what's happened. I know I'm to blame for everything. I don't feel right living at home now, as you can probably understand. But please don't worry about me—I'm staying with a friend, and I'm absolutely fine. I promise I'll call you as soon as I feel ready.
>
> I love you all—and again, I'm so, so sorry.
>
> Love,
> Elizabeth

"Don't you want to tell them who the friend is?" Enid wondered. "It's really going to upset them if they don't know exactly where you are."

Elizabeth shook her head. "I don't want them to know. If they do, they'll feel they have to call up and ask me to come back. No, this way's much better."

"OK," Enid said and sighed. She picked up the two copies of the letter Elizabeth had printed out. "You want me to come with you to deliver these? If anyone's there, I can sneak up and slip the letters into the mailboxes so you won't have to see them."

"That would be wonderful," Elizabeth said gratefully.

She couldn't believe how supportive Enid was being. As soon as they had gotten back from the café to the Rollinses' house, Enid had explained everything to her mother and asked if Elizabeth could stay with them for a while.

"As long as you let your parents know where you are so they won't be worried," Mrs. Rollins had said.

But Elizabeth wasn't quite ready to do that—not yet. Eventually she would let them know, but for the moment she needed to cut herself off completely. It would be easier for her—and for all of them—that way, she decided.

Eleven

Jessica was *not* in a good mood when she got home early Friday evening.

First of all, for the first time in as long as she could remember, she didn't have a single thing planned for the weekend. Nobody had asked her out, unless she counted Charlie. And Jessica definitely did not count him, not since she had found out what a jerk he was.

To make her situation even worse, that afternoon there had been a Pi Beta Alpha meeting to discuss plans for the big costume party coming up in exactly one week. The social committee had been working hard, and it looked like the party was going to be fantastic. They had lined up a band, and they had all sorts of plans to decorate the gym. And prizes for the best costumes—or best pair of costumes—were being finalized.

But of course everyone was talking about who they were going to bring. Lila had just met a guy at a dance class she was taking, and she was going to ask him. Amy didn't have a date yet, but she was planning on asking someone she had met in her tennis class. Cara, of course, was going with Steven. That meant Jessica was the only one without a date. It was demoralizing. Completely, totally demoralizing. Jessica had to find a wonderful date—fast. But where?

All these thoughts were buzzing through her head as she opened the front door of the house at five-thirty on Friday evening. The house was dark—and quiet.

"Liz?" Jessica called.

There was no answer.

Jessica's rotten mood grew even worse. Her twin was probably off with some gorgeous guy like Paul, Jessica thought, and she probably planned on sticking *her* with all the predinner chores. Well, Jessica had no intention of acting like a scullery maid for her sister. As a matter of fact, she knew exactly what she could do to make herself feel better. Maybe she could even find a date!

With one stealthy glance at the door to make sure nobody was approaching, Jessica made a dive for the telephone. She knew the teen party line number by heart.

"Jessica!" Sara cried when she recognized Jessica's voice. "Where have you been? You haven't called in ages!"

"My mom got the phone bill, and I haven't been allowed to anymore." Jessica tried to visualize Sara, whom she had spoken to many times on the party line a few weeks back. Was Sara at all like she seemed on the phone? Or was she as different in person as Charlie was?

Within seconds she'd made sure that Charlie wasn't on the line. In fact, none of the voices except Sara's was familiar.

"Have you talked to Charlie," Jessica asked Sara, "since Wednesday?" She couldn't resist hearing what Charlie had been saying about her.

"Yeah, I've talked to him, all right." Sara giggled. "Probably more recently than you have."

Jessica was confused. "Did he say anything about the two of us meeting?"

"He can't talk about anything else," Sara confirmed. "But, Jessica, there's something you should know—and I'm going to take a chance and tell you, since Charlie never will. That guy you had those dates with—he wasn't Charlie."

"What?" Jessica said, stunned. "Are you kidding me?"

"I'm telling you the truth, I promise. Charlie's afraid you won't think he's good-looking enough, so he got a friend of his to go in his place. From the way he described it, though, it doesn't sound like his plan worked very well." Sara giggled. "He said Brook is kind of boring. Cute, but boring."

"He's got that right," Jessica said, still flabbergasted. "So you mean he told you all about this? What did he say?"

"Well, he didn't think he had a choice. He told me that he stalled you as long as he could, but you made it seem like you wouldn't talk to him anymore if you two didn't meet." Sara cleared her throat. "Only it doesn't sound like *meeting* made you want to keep talking to him, either."

"Yeah, but that wasn't Charlie I met. That was just some friend of his." Now Jessica was dying of curiosity. Who *was* the real Charlie Ryan?

"You're not going to like him if you meet him, Jess. He said so himself. He just isn't the tall, dark, and handsome type," Sara concluded.

"Have you seen him?" Jessica demanded.

"No. But I could tell he was serious about this. He's been so upset, he won't even call the line anymore."

Jessica shook her head in amazement.

Was it true that he wasn't good-looking, or was he just incredibly shy?

She was about to ask Sara another question when the front door opened and Mrs. Wakefield came in. "Listen, I'll talk to you later," Jessica said hastily, hanging up without another word.

She knew she would be in big trouble if she got caught using the party line. As it was, she would be in enough trouble when her mother got the bill. But it had been worth it. At least she had learned that the Charlie she knew and liked wasn't a jerk!

"It's not like Liz to be this late and not call," Alice Wakefield said anxiously. It was seven o'clock, and she had brought home Chinese food for dinner. Steven was back from Cara's, and Jessica, who was starving, kept opening cartons and sampling the contents. But Elizabeth was nowhere to be seen.

"I hope this doesn't have anything to do with what happened last night," Steven said, giving Jessica a concerned look.

Jessica could have killed Steven. Why did he have to bring that up in front of their mother?

"What happened last night?" Mrs. Wakefield asked, looking from one to the other.

"Nothing," Jessica said.

But at exactly the same minute Steven said, "Well, we kind of got in a fight . . . well, not a fight, exactly. But everyone was mad at everyone else, and somehow Jessica and I ended up accusing Elizabeth of having . . ." His voice trailed off.

"Having what?" Mrs. Wakefield asked, her voice rising a little.

"Uh—sort of—having caused you and Dad to break up," Steven finished uneasily.

"*What?*" Mrs. Wakefield stared at him in horror. "Did I hear what you said, or am I going crazy?"

"Mom, come on, it *was* her fault, at least partly," Jessica defended herself. "Liz was the one who went and blabbed the phone number of the inn at Tahoe to Julia. If it weren't for that, you and Daddy would never have gotten in that big fight, and you'd still be together!"

Alice Wakefield's eyes flashed angrily. "I see," she said stiffly. "And is this—this theory of yours, something you actually shared with your sister?"

"Well, kind of," Jessica admitted slowly.

"We didn't exactly mean to," Steven added. "But one thing led to another, we were all angry . . ."

Mrs. Wakefield shook her head. "Liz must be going out of her mind! You know how sensitive she is about things like that! If she really believes that she had anything to do with our decision to separate—"

Steven jumped to his feet. "Hey, what was that? Did you hear someone at the front door?" He raced into the foyer. "Maybe it's Liz!"

But there was nobody at the door and nobody outside, either. All he saw was an unfamiliar car pulling away from the curb. He was about to shut the door when he spotted something on the edge of the stoop. It was a plain white envelope addressed, "Mom, Steven, and Jessica."

Steven hurried back into the kitchen. "It's from Liz," he said, passing the envelope to his mother. "Look—it's her handwriting!"

Jessica and Steven watched in stunned silence as their mother opened the envelope and read the letter inside.

By eight-thirty the Wakefield household was in a state of chaos. Mrs. Wakefield was sitting at the kitchen table, holding the telephone in her hands. She had already dialed the numbers of every single one of Elizabeth's friends, but no one knew where Elizabeth was. Enid's number, which she tried first, had been busy for an hour, and there was nobody home at Todd's house.

"Where can she be?" Mrs. Wakefield cried, looking at Steven and Jessica in anguish.

Jessica was close to tears. "It's my fault. I was

the one who kept blaming her. But I had no idea she'd do something this crazy! She can't just move out of the house!"

Steven paced back and forth. "If only we'd all been able to talk to each other instead of fighting," he said sadly.

Just then, the front door burst open. All three Wakefields jumped up, their expressions brightening.

"Liz?" Mrs. Wakefield cried.

But it wasn't Elizabeth. It was Ned Wakefield, waving a letter in his hand.

"Where is she? What happened to her?" he cried.

"Oh, Ned," Mrs. Wakefield said, slumping back in her chair. "We thought you might be Liz."

"Tell me what happened," he urged. "All I know is that when I got home from work, this letter was in my mailbox. I came straight over here the minute I read it."

"Let me see your letter," Mrs. Wakefield said, snatching it out of his hand. Her face fell as she read it. "It's the same as mine."

"Have you tried calling all her friends? Enid? Todd?" Mr. Wakefield asked.

Mrs. Wakefield nodded. "Yes. Enid's line is busy, and Todd isn't home. Ned, I feel absolutely awful. The kids have been telling me that

Elizabeth feels she's to blame for us splitting up."

Mr. Wakefield sank down into one of the kitchen chairs. "I just don't see how," he said. "Did any of us ever give her that impression?"

Jessica started to speak up, but Mrs. Wakefield silenced her. "The truth is, none of us has been able to communicate at all for the past few months. Ned, you and I have been fighting terribly. But we've been hurting our children as well as ourselves." She turned to Jessica and Steven. "Liz couldn't have gotten the feeling that she was to blame just from the remarks you two made last night. I think it's high time we stopped blaming one another and started looking for ways to make repairs."

Everyone was quiet for a minute. "If only Liz were here," Jessica said morosely.

"We'll find her," Mr. Wakefield said, putting his arm around her waist. "And when we do, I think we've all got a lot of talking to do. Your mother is right," he added, looking at Mrs. Wakefield with warmth and understanding. "It's time for all of us to talk—really talk. We can't work miracles overnight, but we do need to start working things through. And I think that we're all ready to try."

Friday night actually ended up being rather fun for Elizabeth. She and Enid stayed up until almost two in the morning, watching videos on the TV in Enid's bedroom. Mrs. Rollins had set up a cot for Elizabeth with a cozy quilt and two down pillows. And Elizabeth felt good, talking things through with her friend. Until coming to the Rollinses', she hadn't realized how much of a strain her family had been living under. At Enid's house everything felt relaxed and easy. There was no arguing, no pressure.

"Hey, tell me something," Enid said when the romantic comedy they had been watching ended. "Do you miss Todd, or are you glad it's over between the two of you?"

Elizabeth looked thoughtfully at her friend before answering. "I do miss him," she said at last. "You know, it was a strange feeling going out on dates this week. I kind of enjoyed the novelty, but they got boring pretty fast. It was fun going out with Paul, but he and I didn't have a single thing to talk about. And seeing Steve and John . . ." Elizabeth shrugged. "I didn't feel anything special when I was with them. Not like I did with Todd, anyway."

"He misses you, too. Do you know how many times he's asked me about you?"

Elizabeth turned away and said angrily, "He doesn't miss me! I've seen him three times this week with that really cute sophomore named Allison—the one with the short red hair and a great figure." She stood up and pushed the rewind button. "Forget it, Enid. Todd and I are history. I'll just have to get used to it."

"Why get used to it? Why not do something about it?" Enid asked.

"It's better this way," Elizabeth insisted stubbornly. "Look, what possible good could have come out of my relationship with Todd? All that would happen is that we'd break up when we went away to college." Elizabeth shrugged. "What's the point of staying together when we're only going to split up in a year?"

"That's crazy," Enid said. "I don't know, Liz. For someone who used to have a lot of common sense, you've sure been coming up with some weird ideas lately. What about the fact that you and Todd love each other, that you enjoy each other's company? Isn't that good enough?"

Elizabeth took a deep breath. "No," she said softly, "it isn't."

She didn't know how to put it into words, but she felt very strongly that some kinds of pain were avoidable. If she could have written that exam for Mr. Collins, she would have said that she agreed love was fragile—so fragile people shouldn't let themselves feel it, unless they knew for certain they wouldn't get hurt.

Maybe that wasn't what the great authors had said. They thought people should love no matter what, love and take risks, love and feel the whole range of emotions.

But Elizabeth knew better. She wasn't going to open her heart to somebody just so he could stomp all over it. And she didn't want to hurt anybody else the way she had hurt her family and Todd. Getting involved with people and caring about them was just too risky.

Yes, she missed Todd. She missed him terribly. But she wasn't going to risk asking him to come back to her. Not when she believed, deep down, that even true love didn't have a chance of surviving.

"You really left the phone off the hook? All night?" Enid demanded.

"I know it was awful, but I had to. I needed a night without my family calling, and I knew they'd call your house first," Elizabeth confessed.

It was Saturday morning, and she was waiting for her mother to come pick her up. Not even ten o'clock, Elizabeth mused, and her mother had already found her!

"I had a feeling you were there," was all her mother said when she finally got through to the Rollinses' home that morning. That was it. She didn't yell or make any accusations. She said, "Are you ready to come home now?"

"Yes—I think so," Elizabeth said slowly.

She had no idea what to expect when she got home. But she knew she couldn't hide at Enid's house forever. And just one night away from home had made her realize how important it was for her to resolve things with her parents and her brother and sister.

However confused and upset she was feeling, she knew one thing for sure: Her family mattered more to her than anything else in the world. And if they were willing to talk about the problems, she had to be able to do the same thing.

Twelve

Elizabeth took a deep breath. "This is kind of hard," she told her mother, who opened the front door of the Wakefield house.

"It's hard for me, too. For all of us," Alice Wakefield said, giving her daughter's shoulder a squeeze. The loving smile on her face gave Elizabeth the courage to walk in through the foyer to the living room.

To her astonishment her father was the first person she saw. "Liz!" he cried, stepping forward and lifting her off the ground in a huge bear hug. "I'm so glad you're all right! You had me scared out of my wits," he whispered, stroking her hair.

Elizabeth rested her head on his shoulder. It

felt nice to be hugged. Steven rushed up and tried to give her a hug, too. And even though Jessica hung back a little, Elizabeth could tell from the look on her face that her sister was glad to see her.

"I'm sorry we said that stuff to you, Liz," Steven said in a low voice.

Elizabeth reddened. "You only said what you felt."

"That's not really true. I wasn't angry at you, but at the whole situation," Steven protested. "I didn't mean it."

"I think we all need to sit down and talk this thing through," Mr. Wakefield cut in. "Liz, you have no idea how terrible we all felt last night. As soon as we realized that you thought your mother and I had decided to live apart for a while because of you—"

"We were hysterical," Mrs. Wakefield added. "And the truth is, Liz, we know you weren't just being paranoid." She smiled. "Sensitive, as always, but not paranoid. There's been so much anger and blame around here that none of us really knows what to think or feel anymore."

"I guess I shouldn't have said that stuff," Jessica muttered. "I didn't mean to, Lizzie. I was just really upset." She coughed. "And I know it wasn't your fault. Mom and Dad split up because of stuff going on between them, not because of us."

"That's right," Mr. Wakefield said forcefully. "Listen, I guess we didn't handle this very well a few weeks back. Your mother and I were both so upset ourselves that we didn't do a very good job of talking it out with the three of you. Neither of us bothered to explain to you why we were temporarily separating." He looked sadly at his wife. "Your mother and I knew we weren't getting along the way we wanted to. We knew we each needed some time apart. And we thought this was the best way to handle it."

Elizabeth stared down at the carpet. How long would her parents need to be apart? Did her father really mean it when he said the separation was temporary? These were questions that she needed answered. But she had a feeling her parents didn't know the answers, either—not yet, anyway.

Mr. Wakefield smiled at her. He looked tired, but his eyes were full of feeling. "We're all just going to have to be patient with one another," he said, as if reading Elizabeth's mind. "But your mother and I both hope that all of you will be open about your feelings. It's only natural that every one of us will feel some guilt and anger about this. We just need to make sure we get those feelings out so we can deal with them.

It's keeping them bottled up inside that makes us go crazy and start thinking things that aren't true," he said, looking at Elizabeth.

Elizabeth felt a wave of relief wash over her. "So you guys would've decided to live apart anyway . . . even if I hadn't given Julia the number of the place in Tahoe?"

"Oh, sweetheart," her mother cried, throwing her arms around her. "You weren't to blame for anything! You were only trying your hardest to keep us together!"

Elizabeth sighed heavily. For the first time in weeks, she didn't feel numb anymore.

She felt as if her heart were breaking, both with joy and pain. She loved her family *so* much. And she so desperately wanted her parents to live together again and to be happy.

At the same time Elizabeth had learned something she would never forget. Her parents had their own lives, apart from her, and she wasn't responsible for what happened between them. That was scary, because it meant that she didn't have any control over what happened between them in the future. But it also meant that she could stop feeling responsible for their decisions.

And I can start figuring my own life out, a little voice inside her said.

"It's nice to be home," Elizabeth said, smiling tentatively.

"Who wants some lunch?" Mrs. Wakefield asked.

"I do," Jessica said. "I'm starving!"

"Good, then you won't mind helping out," her mother said.

"It's not my turn!" Jessica protested.

Steven put his arm around Elizabeth's shoulder. "What were you saying about it being nice to be home?"

"So, what are you doing tonight?" Jessica asked, throwing herself across the bottom of her sister's bed and knocking three books to the floor in the process. Elizabeth was sitting on the bed, leaning against the headboard, trying to do some homework.

"I don't know," she said, reaching over the side of the bed to pick up the books, "I think Enid and I might go see a movie."

"What about Todd?" Jessica demanded.

"What about him?" Elizabeth asked.

"Come on, Liz. When are you going to admit how much you miss him?" Jessica asked.

Elizabeth laughed. "You really get right to the point, don't you, Jess?"

"There's no time for beating around the bush. You've already almost blown it with him, and as your twin sister I feel I should be the one to tell you that," Jessica stated firmly.

Elizabeth stared into space. As a matter of fact, she had been thinking about Todd non-stop for the past few days. She wondered if he still missed her, as Enid had said. She doubted it—she had been too mean to him.

"He's probably off somewhere with Allison," Elizabeth said and shrugged. She wasn't going to let Jessica know how much she cared. Some things needed to be kept private!

"You mean you're not even going to try and make up with him?" Jessica gave her sister an indignant look. "Come on, Liz. You know you two are the perfect couple. You're just like Romeo and Juliet," she added.

"Yeah, well, look what happened to them," Elizabeth reminded her sister. "Now do me a favor and get out of here, OK? I'm working on something I owe Mr. Collins."

But even after Jessica left the room, Elizabeth sat and stared out the window for a long time. She couldn't stop thinking about Todd.

If only there was some way to let him know how much she still cared for him.

"She's gone crazy, Steve," Jessica announced the next day.

She and her brother were sitting out by the pool. A truce had definitely settled over the Wakefield household. Mr. Wakefield had come over that morning for brunch, and everyone had been in great spirits. But there were still a few things that were bothering Jessica, namely, her sister's reluctance to get back together with Todd.

"Listen, we really owe Liz a favor. After all, we made her miserable last week. The least we could do is a little matchmaking," Jessica suggested.

"What do you mean?" Steven asked.

"Liz really wants to get back together with Todd, I'm sure of it. And I know for a fact that Todd misses her. Amy told me, and she ought to know. She tried to get him to go out with her all last week."

"So what's the problem?" Steven said. "Why don't they just kiss and make up?"

"Because!" Jessica said impatiently. "Liz is afraid Todd doesn't like her anymore, and Todd feels too rejected to make the first move."

"Oh," Steven said, tapping his sunglasses against his leg.

"Obviously what they need is someone to get them together," Jessica continued.

"Uh-oh," Steven moaned. "I hate it when you get that look in your eyes, Jess. Tell me you're not thinking what I think you are."

"I just feel we owe Liz something, after all the suffering we put her through," Jessica said lightly.

"And I suppose you have just the plan," Steven said, rolling his eyes.

"I sure do," Jessica said. "You know there's a

big costume party coming up at school this Friday night, right?"

"Sure. In fact, I'm being dragged to it. Cara really wants to go." Steven grimaced. "We haven't figured out our costumes yet."

"Well, let's say you and I come up with some great way to get Liz and Todd together before the costume party. That way they can be reunited in front of the whole school." Jessica's eyes were shining. "And you and I can get all the credit!"

"OK, Jess, I'll help," Steven said slowly. "Tell me how you plan to arrange this reunion."

Jessica could barely contain her excitement. "I'll tell you the whole thing. But you have to promise to cooperate all the way down to the last detail!"

"I'll probably regret this, but go ahead," Steven said with a sigh.

Elizabeth was busy finishing an article for *The Oracle* on Sunday afternoon. She was so busy that she barely noticed when Jessica barged into her room, claiming she wanted to borrow some perfume.

A minute later Jessica was back out in the hallway. "OK. She's wearing blue jeans, a white cotton sweater, and has her hair back in a french braid." She shook her head. *Boring*, she thought.

If only her twin had chosen a better outfit, especially since Jessica had to impersonate her!

Ten minutes later she was dressed in clothing identical to her sister's. From the phone in her bedroom she dialed Todd's number.

"Todd, it's me—Elizabeth," she said, holding the phone away from her mouth so he couldn't hear her voice well enough to recognize it.

"Liz?" he said, sounding very surprised.

"Can I see you this afternoon? There's something important I have to talk to you about," Jessica said in her best impersonation of Elizabeth's voice.

"I guess so," Todd said uncertainly.

"Can you meet me at the picnic tables at Secca Lake in an hour?" Jessica asked.

"Uh, sure," Todd answered.

"Great! See you then." Jessica winked at Steven, who had just come into her bedroom, and gave him a thumbs-up sign.

Everything was going perfectly. All systems go!

"Now, remember," Jessica instructed Steven after she had hung up the phone. "You have to get Liz to come with you, even if she insists she has too much homework. I'll get there first and start talking to Todd, but you should time it so you two arrive about five minutes later. We'll be at the fourth picnic table. Just kind of stroll up and get Liz to listen to what we're saying."

Jessica grinned. "I'll find some way to interrupt the conversation and run back to the car, and then you and I can convince her to trade places with me." She giggled. "What could be simpler?"

Steven shook his head. "I still think you're nuts," he said. But he agreed to go ahead with the plan.

An hour later, Jessica was waiting for Todd at the fourth picnic table under the trees at Secca Lake. *I hope this works,* she thought. *If not, Liz will never forgive us!*

"Liz?" Todd said in a tentative voice, coming up behind her.

He seemed nervous. Jessica gave him a warm, encouraging smile.

"Hi," she said softly.

Todd stared at her. "Are you OK? You—I don't know—you don't look like you feel very well."

Thanks a lot, Todd, Jessica thought, furious. *What's wrong with my face?*

"I'm fine," she said sweetly, sinking down onto the bench of the picnic table. Off in the distance she thought she heard a car. She hoped it was Steven and Elizabeth.

"So, you wanted to talk?" Todd asked her.

Jessica nodded emphatically as she heard a car door shut. She decided to talk quickly so

Todd wouldn't notice her brother and sister arriving. "I've been thinking a lot about what's happened between us, and I want you to know how sorry I am."

"Really?" Todd stared at her. "Are you serious?"

"I was way too hasty," Jessica said. If only she knew a few more details about how Elizabeth and Todd had split up! "I think all the anxiety about my parents was what made me do it. And if you want to get back together . . . well, so do I," she blurted out. Maybe that wasn't the way Elizabeth would have said it, but at least it was direct! "I want to go to the costume party with you," she added.

Todd looked dumbfounded. "Liz, I can't believe my ears. That's wonderful. I mean, well, of course I want to get back together with you! I love you more than anything in the world!"

Jessica heard a telltale snap of a twig behind her. Good—they had eavesdroppers!

"Uh—Todd, hang on one second. I brought something for you, but it's in my car," Jessica stammered. And before he could say another word, she had jumped up and hurried off to the parking lot, which was hidden from the picnic tables by a grove of trees.

Elizabeth was standing behind a tree. Her face was pale, and her expression said it all. She had heard Todd's declaration of love.

"Liz," Jessica said emotionally, "he's waiting for you."

Elizabeth threw her arms around Jessica. "Thank you," she whispered. Her eyes shining, she turned back to her brother. "And thank you, too! Now that I know what you two were up to, I'm sorry I was so obnoxious about going for a walk with you."

"Never mind. You'd better hurry," Steven said, handing her a red rose he'd picked up earlier that afternoon at Jessica's urging. "Todd's waiting."

Elizabeth nodded. And without another word she turned and walked through the trees to join Todd at the picnic table.

"So," Jessica said, turning back to her brother and giving him a big smile. "All's well that ends well!"

Steven shook his head. "Well done, Jess. I have to hand it to you—you really pulled that one off!"

Jessica nodded. "I was pretty spectacular, if I do say so myself."

"But all isn't well yet," Steven reminded her. "Who are *you* planning on going to the costume party with? Or have you forgotten about that?"

Jessica snapped a twig off a tree. "Oh, I don't know," she said airily. "I'll find a date. Listen, we should get out of here before Todd discovers us," she added, hurrying toward Steven's car.

She didn't want to tell Steven about the Charlie Ryan dilemma. The truth was, Jessica was dying for a chance to meet the real Charlie. But what if he wasn't cute at all? Lila and Amy would tease her to death.

We could always go as Beauty and the Beast, she thought, giggling to herself. *Or he could wear a mask and never take it off.*

Suddenly a wonderful idea came to her. Amy had called that morning and said the guy in her tennis class had turned her down. So she didn't have a date, either. Why not get Amy and Charlie, the real Charlie, to go to the dance together as blind dates? Jessica could go with the other Charlie, the handsome one. What was his name, anyway? And the four of them could double-date.

That way Jessica wouldn't be mortified by being caught out in public with someone who wasn't good-looking. And at the same time she would be able to enjoy the benefits of being with both Charlies and having both of them be in love with her! It was the perfect plan!

Thirteen

"So, what do you think of my costume?" Jessica asked Amy, twirling around in front of her full-length mirror.

Jessica thought her costume was fantastic. She had dressed as an intergalactic princess, with lots of foil in her hair and a wonderful silver cape she had borrowed from Lila.

Amy, she couldn't help noticing, was dressed a little on the plain side. Whoever heard of going to a costume party as a cheerleader? She thought it was more than a little corny, especially since everyone at school had seen Amy's cheerleader costume a million times.

But Jessica didn't mind. It just meant she would get even more attention—from both the Charlies!

The double date hadn't been easy to arrange. Jessica had gotten the ball rolling by calling Charlie up and telling him she knew the truth. "You're not the guy who took me roller-skating or out for sushi," she had accused him. "And don't pretend you are, because Sara already told me all about it."

An embarrassed pause had followed her outburst. "OK, I admit it. I sent my friend Brook Atkins in my place to meet you," Charlie finally said.

"Why would you do that?" Jessica demanded, pretending not to know a thing about how shy he was because of his looks. Let Charlie tell her himself. "Don't you like me?"

"Of course I do! It's just . . . well, I knew you were pretty, Jessica. I just had a feeling. And I knew I wouldn't stand a chance once you saw me." Charlie paused. "Brook and I look nothing alike."

Jessica thought about what Charlie had said. So Charlie wasn't good-looking. Well, it didn't mean that they couldn't be friends, she thought. She enjoyed his flattering comments. And who knew? Maybe Charlie had the wrong idea about his looks. Maybe he wasn't really that bad. She was more than prepared to be open-minded, especially since he was going to be Amy's date, not hers.

"Well, listen, I have a big favor to ask of

you," she said, ignoring his comments about his looks. "You introduced me to your friend Brook, right? Well, I have a friend I want to introduce to *you*. How about if the four of us all go to the costume party at Sweet Valley High on Friday night?"

Charlie had refused at first. He said he was too shy. "I don't know, Jessica. I still don't want you to see the real me." But eventually he gave in, after Jessica had pleaded with him for ten minutes.

And now, at last, the long-awaited night was here. Jessica could hardly wait. Both Charlie and Brook would spend the whole night flirting with her, asking her to dance, vying for her attention, she thought. Poor Amy in her cheerleader costume. . . . Well, at least Jessica had provided her friend with a date. Amy had been far too critical of her relationship with Charlie, anyway. This would show her who knew more about dating.

Charlie Ryan came to the costume party as a pirate, and kind of a nice-looking pirate at that, Jessica decided.

True, he wasn't classically handsome. He had a bumpy nose, he was a little too thin, and his eyes were spaced too close together, but there was something very appealing about him. Before the four of them had even gotten to the dance, he had Amy, Jessica, and Brook roaring with laughter. His sense of humor was so dry that Jessica could hardly keep up with him.

And Brook certainly couldn't. Poor Brook. He was as plastic as ever, looking gorgeous in a golfer's sweater, madras pants, and a white cap. "I'm a country-club type," he announced. Jessica had to hide a smile. The costume looked so natural on him!

"What a great costume," Charlie said to Amy, walking around her. "You're a satire of a cheerleader, aren't you?"

"Wh-what?" Amy said, staring uncertainly at him.

"That's the funniest costume I've ever seen. You're a genius," Charlie announced, his brown eyes lighting up.

Jessica frowned. "What about mine?" she demanded.

Charlie laughed. "It's appropriate—a princess dressed as a princess," he said, smiling. But he turned back to Amy. "So how *did* you get the cheerleader idea? Those pom-poms are perfect!"

"Having a good time, Jess?" Elizabeth asked, dancing past with Todd. She looked stunning in her Juliet costume, and Todd, whose face looked more radiant and happy than Jessica had ever seen it, made a wonderful Romeo. *The happy couple, back together at last*, she thought sadly.

"Not really. I thought I had two dates tonight, and it turns out I have none." Jessica pointed across the dance floor to where Charlie and Brook were both talking animatedly to Amy. It was disgusting.

"The pirate's kind of cute," Elizabeth observed.

"I know," Jessica said with a sigh. The more she looked at Charlie, the cuter he seemed— and the less interested he seemed in her. She had no idea why. Hadn't she spent hours twisting her hair up in silver foil? Didn't her cape look wonderful? It was a complete disaster, that's what it was. Here Amy ought to be the one having a miserable time, watching Charlie and Brook fighting for Jessica's attention, and instead the whole thing had backfired!

"You can come dance with us," Elizabeth offered.

Jessica made a face and yanked some of the silver foil out of her hair. "I hate dancing!" she snapped.

"Since when?" Elizabeth asked, smiling.

"I've had it with men. From now on, I'm going to be a completely different person. No more phone lines or dating agencies or crushes or any of that stuff," Jessica declared. "It's too big a waste of time. And anyway, there are much more important things in the world than dances."

Elizabeth gave Jessica a strange look. She was obviously surprised by her sister's change of heart. "Like what?"

"Well, politics, for one thing." Jessica crossed her arms and looked defiant. "You and Steve may not care that Daddy's a serious candidate for mayor of Sweet Valley, but *I* do. I intend to devote every waking minute to helping him with his campaign. If he doesn't win, it isn't going to be on my conscience!"

Elizabeth nodded thoughtfully. "He really does need our help, Jess. You're right. I'm going to see if there's anything I can do after school to help him."

"Me, too," Jessica said emphatically. She was through with boys. From this moment on, every ounce of her energy was going into her father's race for mayor.

Maybe she wouldn't win the stupid costume contest or have a date every Saturday night. But once she was the daughter of the mayor of Sweet Valley, all her friends—and former friends —would be sorry they had ignored her. *Especially* Charlie Ryan and Amy Sutton!

Will Mr. Wakefield really be elected mayor of Sweet Valley? Find out in Sweet Valley High #67 **THE PARENT PLOT.**

COULD *YOU* BE THE NEXT SWEET VALLEY READER OF THE MONTH?

ENTER BANTAM BOOKS' SWEET VALLEY CONTEST & SWEEPSTAKES IN ONE!

Calling all Sweet Valley Fans! Here's a chance to appear in a Sweet Valley book!

We know how important Sweet Valley is to you. That's why we've come up with a Sweet Valley celebration offering exciting opportunities to have YOUR thoughts printed in a Sweet Valley book!

"How do I become a Sweet Valley Reader of the Month?"

It's easy. Just write a one-page essay (no more than 150 words, please) telling us a little about yourself, and why you like to read Sweet Valley books. We will pick the best essays and print them along with the winner's photo in the back of upcoming Sweet Valley books. Every month there will be a new Sweet Valley High Reader of the Month!

And, there's more!

Just sending in your essay makes you eligible for the Grand Prize drawing for a trip to Los Angeles, California! This once-in-a-life-time trip includes round-trip airfare, accommodations for 5 nights (economy double occupancy), a rental car, and meal allowances. (Approximate retail value: $4,500.)

Don't wait! Write your essay today.
No purchase necessary. See the next page for Official rules.

ENTER BANTAM BOOKS' SWEET VALLEY READER OF THE MONTH SWEEPSTAKES

OFFICIAL RULES:

READER OF THE MONTH ESSAY CONTEST

1. <u>No Purchase Is Necessary.</u> Enter by hand printing your name, address, date of birth and telephone number on a plain 3" x 5" card, and sending this card along with your essay telling us about yourself and why you like to read Sweet Valley books to:

READER OF THE MONTH
SWEET VALLEY HIGH
BANTAM BOOKS
YR MARKETING
666 FIFTH AVENUE
NEW YORK, NEW YORK 10103

2. <u>Reader of the Month Contest Winner.</u> For each month from June 1, 1990 through December 31, 1990, a Sweet Valley High Reader of the Month will be chosen from the entries received during that month. The winners will have their essay and photo published in the back of an upcoming Sweet Valley High title.

3. Enter as often as you wish, but each essay must be original and each entry must be mailed in a separate envelope bearing sufficient postage. All completed entries must be postmarked and received by Bantam no later than December 31, 1990, in order to be eligible for the Essay Contest and Sweepstakes. Entrants must be between the ages of 6 and 16 years old. Each essay must be no more than 150 words and must be typed double-spaced or neatly printed on one side of an 8 1/2" x 11" page which has the entrant's name, address, date of birth and telephone number at the top. The essays submitted will be judged each month by Bantam's Marketing Department on the basis of originality, creativity, thoughtfulness, and writing ability, and all of Bantam's decisions are final and binding. Essays become the property of Bantam Books and none will be returned. Bantam reserves the right to edit the winning essays for length and readability. Essay Contest winners will be notified by mail within 30 days of being chosen. In the event there are an insufficient number of essays received in any month which meet the minimum standards established by the judges, Bantam reserves the right not to choose a Reader of the Month. Winners have 30 days from the date of Bantam's notice in which to respond, or an alternate Reader of the Month winner will be chosen. Bantam is not responsible for incomplete or lost or misdirected entries.

4. Winners of the Essay Contest and their parents or legal guardians may be required to execute an Affidavit of Eligibility and Promotional Release supplied by Bantam. Entering the Reader of the Month Contest constitutes permission for use of the winner's name, address, likeness and contest submission for publicity and promotional purposes, with no additional compensation.

5. Employees of Bantam Books, Bantam Doubleday Dell Publishing Group, Inc., and

their subsidiaries and affiliates, and their immediate family members are not eligible to enter the Essay Contest. The Essay Contest is open to residents of the U.S. and Canada (excluding the province of Quebec), and is void wherever prohibited or restricted by law. All applicable federal, state, and local regulations apply.

READER OF THE MONTH SWEEPSTAKES

6. Sweepstakes Entry. No purchase is necessary. Every entrant in the Sweet Valley High, Sweet Valley Twins and Sweet Valley Kids Essay Contest whose completed entry is received by December 31, 1990 will be entered in the Reader of the Month Sweepstakes. The Grand Prize winner will be selected in a random drawing from all completed entries received on or about February 1, 1991 and will be notified by mail. Bantam's decision is final and binding. Odds of winning are dependent on the number of entries received. The prize is non-transferable and no substitution is allowed. The Grand Prize winner must be accompanied on the trip by a parent or legal guardian. Taxes are the sole responsibility of the prize winner. Trip must be taken within one year of notification and is subject to availability. Travel arrangements will be made for the winner and, once made, no changes will be allowed.

7. 1 Grand Prize. A six day, five night trip for two to Los Angeles, California. Includes round-trip coach airfare, accommodations for 5 nights (economy double occupancy), a rental car -- economy model, and spending allowance for meals. (Approximate retail value: $4,500.)

8. The Grand Prize winner and their parent or legal guardian may be required to execute an Affidavit of Eligibility and Promotional Release supplied by Bantam. Entering the Reader of the Month Sweepstakes constitutes permission for use of the winner's name, address, and the likeness for publicity and promotional purposes, with no additional compensation.

9. Employees of Bantam Books, Bantam Doubleday Dell Publishing Group, Inc., and their subsidiaries and affiliates, and their immediate family members are not eligible to enter this Sweepstakes. The Sweepstakes is open to residents of the U.S. and Canada (excluding the province of Quebec), and is void wherever prohibited or restricted by law. If a Canadian resident, the Grand Prize winner will be required to correctly answer an arithmetical skill-testing question in order to receive the prize. All applicable federal, state, and local regulations apply. The Grand Prize will be awarded in the name of the minor's parent or guardian. Taxes, if any, are the winner's sole responsibility.

10. For the name of the Grand Prize winner and the names of the winners of the Sweet Valley High, Sweet Valley Twins and Sweet Valley Kids Essay Contests, send a stamped, self-addressed envelope entirely separate from your entry to: Bantam Books, Sweet Valley Reader of the Month Winners, Young Readers Marketing, 666 Fifth Avenue, New York, New York 10103. The winners list will be available after April 15, 1991.